BETWEEN A ROCK AND A ROYAL

KINGS OF CAROLINA - BOOK 1

SYLVIE STEWART

ROLLING HEARTS PRESS

For Ben
— you may not be a prince, but you're pretty freaking
awesome anyway

CHAPTER ONE

LEO

The clubhead hit the ball with a *thwack*, sending it sailing about two hundred yards down the fairway. Imagining my brother's face imprinted on the ball hadn't hurt.

"Excellent shot, Your Highness."

An eye-roll threatened. This guy had been complimenting every sodding move I'd made all day. I was fairly certain he'd praise the quality of the shit I took if he happened to follow me into the loo. Where in the hell was Malcolm? He was meant to be the one on the receiving end of all this bowing and scraping, not me.

I gave the senator a polite nod and stepped aside, allowing him to tee off. A glance at my phone showed no response to my texts. All I knew was what Malcolm's aide, Alice, had told me this morning—that he was "indisposed" and wouldn't be making the round of golf with the good senator.

Indisposed. Hungover and sandwiched between two naked females was more than likely.

Not for the first time this week, I asked myself how I'd allowed my brother to manipulate me into coming with him on this waste of a trip. It wasn't as if my presence was required. I was the spare. Malcolm was the heir. And what was the purpose of a "goodwill" visit anyway? It seemed to be just another opportunity to waste money and time. I had a life to get back to—important work that needed my attention.

Senator Ames' swing was much more practiced than mine, yet he feigned surprise when his ball landed a good fifty yards past mine. Bad form to show up a prince, no matter how small his country. I was sick of all the bullshit. At least we only had another two days and then we'd be headed back home—back to reality. So, perhaps it wasn't so hard to see why my brother was milking this visit for all it was worth, after all. His life would be changing in a few short weeks.

The senator gestured for me to precede him to the golf carts where our caddies waited. I could have used the walk, but at least this way, we'd be finished more quickly. And then I'd find Malcolm and he could take over. He actually *enjoyed* having his arse kissed.

We finished the round and posed for a few photos before the senator and I parted ways and one of the security personnel took me back to the hotel. The car's cool black leather was heaven, and I let my head fall back while an old Van Morrison song settled over me. Now that I was alone, I could finally breathe.

"You played well, Sir," Andrew commented from the driver's seat.

"For me, I suppose. Thank you, Andrew." I left my response at that and we continued driving in silence. Andrew was keenly attuned to my mood, as was his job, and left me to the music and perfectly conditioned air.

When we arrived at the hotel, I nodded and smiled as graciously as possible to the staff as I stalked to the lifts and boarded the car. I was taken to the top floor and deposited into the penthouse suite where I didn't pause on my mission to find and possibly assault my brother.

One firm push and the double doors to the master bedroom parted, revealing precisely what I had expected. There was Malcolm, bare-chested, dark hair a rumpled mess, lying with his hands behind his head, a half-naked woman on either side of him. I didn't spare the nubile young things more than a passing glance, however. My sights were set.

"Hello, brother dear," Malcolm greeted me with a smug grin, impervious to the daggers I was sending his way.

I heard a gasp before one of the women simpered, "There are two of you!" She moved to climb off the bed, I could only assume to draw me in, but I put a hand out to stop her.

"I'm not the one you want. Believe me, Miss." My jaw was in danger of cracking.

She sat back down awkwardly, and Malcolm stretched an arm out to her. "Don't let Leo scare you away. He's feeling put out today."

I laughed, not finding anything particularly funny. "And I wonder why that would be."

Attention caught on the girl's overly large assets, Malcolm didn't respond. One could only expect so much.

"This is the last time, Mal. We're not schoolboys any longer." My hands went to my hips and I cursed.

Something in my tone must have penetrated, because my brother rose from the bed, thankfully wearing boxers. He excused himself from the women and closed the doors behind us.

"What's all this about anyway? You had a morning of fresh air and conversation. Besides, you know I'm rubbish at golf." He scratched his bare chest and yawned.

I scoffed and turned my back so I wouldn't put him in a chokehold. "I'm done, Malcolm."

He stumbled to the kitchen, no doubt drawn by the enticing scent of coffee drifting our way. "Don't be so dramatic. You're reminding me of Mother."

"Oh, I'm sure she'll have plenty to say about this if she catches wind of it!"

Malcolm palmed a mug and poured the steaming liquid into it. My gaze darted around the space as I realized for the first time that there was no Alice in the suite. In fact, there was no one. Except us and the scantily-clad party guests in the next room.

Reading my mind, he set the mug down and said, "I sent them off to spread some goodwill. The walls are a bit thin here, you know."

I took a breath and closed my eyes for a moment. He wasn't taking any of this seriously. Perhaps it was my fault for letting him get away with whatever he damn well pleased for the last ... well, forever.

Malcolm sighed. "Leo, it's just a round of golf."

"It's not." I moved forward to stand across the raised counter from him. "I'm done masquerading as the goddamn future king, Malcolm. We may look alike, but this is the last time I'm pretending to be you!"

"Good heavens. You need a drink."

Following our confrontation in the kitchen, Malcolm helped the young women dress—apparently, three people and twenty minutes were required for the task—and exit the suite while I helped myself to coffee and checked the messages on my phone. The giggling finally faded as the lift doors closed, and it was just the two of us.

I looked at my brother from my seat at the dining table. He'd donned a t-shirt but still wore just the boxers on his lower half. "It's eleven o'clock. Too early for a drink, I'm afraid." Another message from the Minister of Energy's office popped up on my screen.

"Bite your tongue, Leo. It's never too early for a drink."

"I believe that's precisely what prompted this morning's subterfuge."

He sent me a scolding look.

"Well, of course, we can't forget the dueling vaginas," I added.

His eyebrows spiked and he grinned at my comment. "Never forget a vagina, dear brother."

"My apologies to the girls." I sipped my coffee and we

both examined our phones. We may be royalty, but we're slaves to technology like everyone else.

Malcolm turned his phone screen to me. "See, I could never have looked this chipper that early in the morning." The phone displayed a news photo of me with Senator Ames from the eighteenth green. The headline read, "Prince Malcolm Tees off with Senator Ames." Thankfully it was a small paper that clearly had nothing else to report today.

"Mother will know immediately if she sets eyes on that."

"She's the only one. That's the important thing." He examined the photo again.

"No, the important thing is you taking responsibility for your own duties." I set my phone down on the table. "No matter how much you wish otherwise, you *will* be king, Mal."

He sighed and dropped into the chair across from me. "Can't we pay someone else to do it?"

I spared him a small smile—my first genuine one of the day. Despite my constant frustrations with Malcolm, I wasn't entirely without compassion. "I'm not sure that's how it works."

"Fine." He groaned and dropped his head back.

That made my smile grow. I couldn't help it. This was a battle I'd been fighting for ages, and a very small part of me —all right, maybe not that small—felt a sense of personal satisfaction at the sight of the golden boy not getting his way. Petty, yes. But I'm only human.

His head finally lifted again and he looked me in the

eye. "I'll man up and be as noble as fucking possible." He raised a finger. "On one condition."

I laughed. As if he had a choice. "And what's that?"

"You and I are going on a road trip."

"Absolutely not." She sounded bored, a tone she'd perfected over time, as her word was rarely challenged.

"Mother." I paused, shifting the phone to my other ear.

"I'm well aware of who I am, Leonardo."

It was nails on a chalkboard when she used my full name. I felt as if I should either be inventing an ingenious contraption or standing on the bow of a ship with Kate Winslet.

"He's finally giving in. This is the only thing he's asking for. Can't we please just let him have it? Just a few days and then we'll be on our way home and Malcolm will behave." I almost tripped over the last part. I wasn't in the habit of lying to our mother, but neither was she naïve enough to believe Malcolm's days of mischief would cease so easily.

She sighed, telling me I might be getting somewhere, so I pressed on. "Alice and the team are making arrangements as we speak. All I need is your approval, and we'll get this distraction over with." Malcolm may technically be in charge, but everyone knew that not a thing happened without our mother's consent, making us the only twenty-eight-year-old men on earth who still had to ask their mummy's permission to take a drive. Good lord.

She tutted over the line, and I knew I had her. "Very well. If you must. But, Leonardo, if you're not back by

Sunday, I can't be responsible for what I might do to your brother."

"Understood." It was really the only response I could give. I was expected to be my brother's keeper, whether I chose to or not. "Thank you, Mother."

She made an indecipherable sound. "I don't believe you're the one who should be thanking me. Tell Malcolm to call me or I'll have James donate his Aston Martin to the hospital charity."

My grin was impossible to suppress. She pretended not to have a sense of humor, but it revealed itself from time to time. "I'll be happy to pass that on." Having won approval, the smart thing would have been to get off the phone as soon as humanly possible, but I didn't. "How's Father?"

My mother sighed, but her voice softened when she answered, "Stoic, as usual. He's fine, Leo. Clara is fussing over him at present, but he'll be happy to see you in a few days' time."

With a renewed sense of calm, I said my goodbyes and went in search of Malcolm to share the good news. I finally located him in the closet of his bedroom, holding up two shirts to a contemplative Alice.

"So, you see my dilemma, don't you?"

Her finger pressed against her mouth, her small features pinched in thought. "I do."

The poor girl felt the need to treat all of Malcolm's requests and inquiries with the same degree of intense focus, as if the future of our nation rested on his choice of breakfast meats.

Malcolm raised the hanger holding a gray button-down shirt. "This one says I'm approachable but still have a job to do." The other hanger came up, holding a similar shirt in red. "While this one implies I might be up for a bit of fun once business is taken care of."

I thought they both said he was a pain in the arse, but I kept my mouth shut.

Was it my imagination, or did Alice color a bit when Malcolm alluded to his extracurricular activities? Not possible. She was more than accustomed to the revolving door on Malcolm's bedroom. And, besides, she was engaged to be married to some banker, I believed.

"The gray one," I interjected, hands in the pockets of my trousers. "Red only brings out the broken capillaries in your eyes from your excessive drinking."

Malcolm turned, noticing me for the first time, and then nodded back to Alice. "Good point. Make a note, Alice. Take all red clothing and have it destroyed."

She nodded back, tucking a strand of dark hair behind her ear. "Absolutely, Sir." She swept past me and I gave her a polite smile which she returned.

"And fetch me some eyedrops if you would, love!" Malcolm called out after her. He gave the red shirt a disgusted look and tossed it to the corner of the closet. "So, did the *Grande Dame* give her consent?"

I nodded once. "She did. But only two extra days, Mal. Then it's back to reality."

He frowned. "Two days? How are we expected to see everything in two days?"

My brows drew together, an uneasy sensation crawling over me. Exactly what had he planned? "You said you wanted to see the mountains. Surely two days is sufficient time for that."

He nodded absently, lost in thought for a moment. Then he shook his head as if to clear it, and a grin appeared. "Not to worry. We'll make it work." He patted my shoulder on his way past me to the bedroom, leaving me to wonder exactly what I'd just signed myself up for.

Two days later, with meetings and appearances completed, I found myself tucked in the backseat of a luxury BMW next to my brother. Alice rode in front with Trevor, the head of Malcolm's security team, and another massive vehicle trailed behind with two more security personnel. All other staff had been sent home while we embarked on our trip to West Virginia, of all places. I hadn't heard flattering things, but I was willing to suspend judgment. Perhaps it was like a soft cheese—at first, all you notice is the stench, but it's really quite lovely once you try it.

"I'm particularly looking forward to the moonshine," Malcolm said, peering out the window as the view transitioned from flowering trees and historical monuments to clusters of retail parks and petrol stations.

Unbeknownst to the rest of us, Malcolm had been harboring a dream since childhood to follow the path set forth by John Denver in the perennial favorite "Country Roads." Of course, *I* knew that was complete bollocks. Malcolm's only childhood dreams had consisted of fast cars and learning the combination to the cupboard where Ms. Fauntleroy kept the chocolates. I should know—I'd been the one to help him pick the lock. No one seemed prepared to challenge him, so off we went to find the Blue Ridge

Mountains and Shenandoah River. (Allow me to apologize for putting the song in your head on constant replay.)

"I've heard moonshine can cause brain damage, Sir." Alice's concerned voice warned.

Malcolm merely smiled.

I unbuttoned my coat and repositioned myself in the leather seat. "I'm not sure there's much left to damage, Alice."

She sent me a scolding look over her shoulder. Her devotion to Malcolm was unshakable and often made me smile.

"Don't you worry, love. I've been in training for this," Malcolm reassured.

I shook my head at my brother and he ignored me. If I were being honest, this side trip had its advantages. At least there would be no need to pose for photographs and engage in our public personas. Outside of Washington, I doubted anyone even knew who we were—even in the capital, for that matter, we were practically invisible. It wasn't as if we were media darlings like William and Harry, thank Christ. I doubted ninety-nine percent of the world's population could locate the Feldlands on a map.

"We've arranged for a stay at the Virginia estate of Congresswoman Eldridge. Her staff is expecting us for dinner, so we'll quickly cross over into West Virginia and come back down for the evening." Alice tapped into her phone and passed two bottles of cold Perrier to us, ever the efficient multi-tasker.

Malcolm cursed under his breath. "That won't do at all. The entire purpose of this break is to have an *authentic* experience. We can't do that by popping into West

Virginia, taking a bloody selfie, and then talking weather and politics with Congresswoman fucking Eldridge and her husband!"

Part of me agreed with my brother—it did sound about as exciting as watching Alice arrange Malcolm's cutlery. But I also understood the need to be cautious. It was a minor miracle we'd been given the leeway to arrange the trip at all.

Alice sputtered from the front seat, tucking her hair behind her ears nervously. That poor girl deserved a raise for dealing with my boor of a brother twenty-odd hours of each day.

"What exactly had you expected, Malcolm? Did you think we'd bunk in a camper on top of a mountain?"

He huffed and turned his head to the window again. "Maybe," I heard him mutter.

Surely there was some compromise to be made, although I knew it would be difficult at best on such short notice. I took in Malcolm's profile, noticing for the first time the bags under his eyes and the frown lines etching themselves into his cheek. He looked tired, and maybe even a bit lost.

Bugger.

Knowing I'd regret it immediately, I opened my mouth anyway.

"I think I have an idea."

CHAPTER TWO

RUBY

"Well, isn't that just freaking perfect!?" I jammed the lock to the bay door in place and seriously considered taking up homicide as my new hobby. A girl needs a good pastime.

"I'm so sorry, baby girl." My uncle came up behind me and put a hand on my shoulder. That in itself told me how awful the situation was. Carl was not a toucher.

I scrubbed my hands over my face, not giving one single shit that I was probably smearing grease all over my skin. Carl's mouth pulled down in a defeated frown when I turned, his furrowed brow making his overgrown eyebrows join together like a gray caterpillar edging its way across his face. A sigh escaped me. My plan to strangle my cousin would have to wait for a second, but that boy had best prepare to kiss his nuts goodbye.

"It's not your fault, Uncle Carl." I pressed my lips together in a tight line to keep myself from screaming.

One hand scratched at the back of his neck. "Yes, it is. I didn't have to bail him out." He shook his head. "I should have known better."

Well, he was not wrong on that, but I really didn't blame him. What other choice do you have when your son gets arrested and is facing a prison sentence? It doesn't matter much that the idiot deserved to be incarcerated for the rest of his damn life. When he begged Carl to bail him out, I knew the old man wouldn't be able to say no. Carl is a great dad. Hell, he's the only dad *I've* ever known. Which just made me even more pissed off that Jason gave us all the big old "fuck you" and skipped bail, not caring one single bit what that would mean for the rest of us.

Carl is many things, but a thinking man, he's not. Give him an engine to overhaul or an asshole to punch in the face, and Carl's your guy. But he's not one for thinking past immediate consequences. If he was, he would have seen this coming from a mile away. Freakin' Jason.

I paced over to one of the rolling carts and started putting tools away, my hands needing something to do. "We've got to find a way out of this. Tell me exactly what they said."

Carl followed me and reached into the back pocket of his Carhartts to pull out a folded sheet of paper. The once-white note was marred with black streaks from Carl's hands. "It just outlines the contract I signed and the fact that we're now screwed. If we can get Jason back, we can work something out, but I haven't got the first clue where he went."

Like his dad, Jason is also not a thinking man. But he has more "associates" than I can count, so there was no clear place to start. I shook my head. "We'll have to leave that part to the police." Turning to my uncle, I crossed my arms and eyed him. "And I'm trusting that you're gonna let his ass swing for this one, Uncle Carl. No more letting him guilt you. He made his bed and he needs to lie in it, no matter that it'll be inside the state pen."

"I know." His voice was quiet, and I felt a twinge of guilt for lecturing him. But somebody had to. Carl's heart was almost as big as his beer gut, God bless the man.

"Okay, go on. What else does it say?" I gestured to the unfolded paper.

He narrowed his eyes at the letter. "Uh, since I put the garage up as collateral, if they don't get the boy back and we don't come up with the money in the next sixty days we forfeit the place." Carl cursed and folded the paper again.

A rock settled in my gut and my head got light. Sixty days. *Shit.* This was becoming way too real. Not that I hadn't gotten the gist of the situation before, but hearing it out loud was a kick in the ass. And it wasn't just my livelihood that was at stake here. My apartment was part of the building as well. I was going to be homeless thanks to my selfish asshole of a cousin.

Unless ...

Carl eyed me, his head beginning to shake like his hair was on fire. "Don't even think about it!" His booming voice echoed through the carport.

My hands hit my hips. "I'll bet I can get a good 20K for her!" I protested.

"You are *not* selling Stella!" He poked me with his

index finger and I pushed it out of my way, leaning in toward him.

"I can do whatever I want, Uncle Carl. She's *my* car!" My car I'd poured my heart and soul into. Not to mention all my damn money.

He growled at me—freaking growled! "It ain't even gonna help, Ruby! Where are we gonna get the rest?"

"We'll figure it out. There are other things we can sell."

His hands flew up in exasperation. "I already sold just about every damn thing I had to pay the bail deposit. And you know good and well any profits went to Sadie's tuition!" He wedged himself between the cart and me and picked up where I'd left off. It seemed I wasn't the only one who needed an outlet. A couple wrenches landed in a drawer, the clanging sound bouncing off the walls of the garage.

I stepped aside. "So you're just gonna give up and hand over the keys?" That didn't sound like the Carl I knew.

He spared me a glance. "I didn't say that. We'll figure something else out. We've got time."

Good gracious! "You think thirty thousand dollars is just going to pop up out of the blue in the next two months? You're delusional, old man!"

I turned to walk out before I said something I'd regret. The banging stopped and Carl's voice halted me, the tone so quiet I almost didn't hear it. "Please, baby girl." Despite everything that made me who I am, I felt my eyes get wet. My back was turned, so he didn't see, thank Christ. "I'll find a way. Just give me some time."

I took a deep breath and let it out slowly. It would take

a bit to get the right buyer for Stella, and this was Carl, who never asked me for anything. If it meant that much to him, I could give him a little time.

"Okay," I responded, not turning around. "But we're not losing the garage, no matter what it takes, Uncle Carl. I'll give you a couple weeks, and then I'm putting feelers out on Stella."

"Fair enough." He sounded like he was walking to his execution.

Did I mention I was gonna kill my cousin?

My boots stomped on the stairs to my apartment, and I didn't even bothering taking them off when I entered. The dirty floors would be someone else's problem soon if we didn't figure this shit out anyway. I stalked to the fridge where I pulled out a cold can of Pepsi, not that my heart needed the kickstart. My butt leaned into the counter and I tapped my dirty nails on the surface. There had to be a solution.

Too bad Sadie hadn't graduated already. She was in her senior year at App State, majoring in finance. If only she were bringing in a paycheck, we could maybe get a loan or something. Not that we'd be bothering her about this. The first thing she'd do is run home to K-ville and do her best to save the day. Well, that's not *exactly* true. The first thing she'd do is find her douchebag brother and kick his ass to Raleigh and back for putting us in this position. I almost felt sorry for him. How the two of them came from the same womb was beyond me, and I was almost grateful that my aunt wasn't here to see what her dumbass offspring had done.

My phone vibrated in my pocket and I pulled it out to see that Sadie must have been reading my damn mind.

Sadie: *Hey, girl. You okay?*

It was almost eerie how well she knew me.

Me: *I'm good. How are classes?*

Sadie: *Almost over, thank God! Only six more weeks!*

I was so freaking proud of her—and so was everybody else. That girl would have the world at her feet one of these days. Despite the current shitstorm, I smiled and typed my response.

Me: *You're going to kick ass on your exams, woman!*

Sadie: *You know it. So, how's Dad?*

Crap. I took a sip of my drink and mentally crossed my fingers. It sucked lying to her.

Me: *He's good. You worry about you. I've got Uncle Carl.*

Sadie: *I know, but I still feel bad I'm not there. It's not every day your son faces prison.*

I choked out a half-laugh with no trace of humor. *Or skips bail and screws over the whole family.* Not that I was telling her that. As far as Sadie knew, her brother had been arrested for armed robbery and was currently hunkered down at her dad's place awaiting his final court appearances. And I wasn't about to alter her reality one iota.

Me: *Girl, you know it was just a matter of time.*

Sadie: *I am so done with him!*

Me: *You and me both. No more talk about the evil spawn! You got any hot mountain-man prospects up there?*

We couldn't continue on the topic or I'd risk tipping her off. I chugged the rest of the soda and threw the can in a perfect arc to the recycle bin in the corner. Two points!

Sadie: *Please! I'm too busy for guys.*

Ha! She was never too busy for guys. She just hadn't found one worth her time yet.

Me: *Liar.*

Sadie: *Shit! I gotta go or I'm gonna miss my study group.*

That might have been a copout on her part, but I had things to do too.

Me: *Go kick some financial ass!*

Sadie: *I will. Love you!*

Me: *Love you more.*

I tossed the phone to the counter, still feeling restless. I'd meant what I said to Carl. He'd get a couple weeks, but that didn't mean I was just going to sit on my ass. What I needed was a shower and trip down to Benny's.

Bars like Benny's were a dime a dozen, or at least that's how it appeared at first glance, but it couldn't be further from the truth. I mean, honestly, how many bars had an original Wurlitzer 1015 and a wooly mammoth head mounted above the bar (the latter probably not so original)?

"Hey, look who's here! What can I get you, darlin'?" Benny himself made his way to the end of the bar as I approached. I couldn't help but smile at him. Benny only had two moods: cheerful as hell and pissed the fuck off. Luckily, I always got the cheerful side. I'd seen the pissed off side and was happy to never be on the receiving end. It was usually reserved for out-of-towners who didn't know any better or drunks who made the mistake of messing with one of Benny's waitresses. Or his jukebox.

"Just a Pepsi for now, thanks. How's it going, Benny?"

"Can't complain." His bald head reflected the colored bar lights as he bent to fill my glass with ice. "Heard about Jason." He shook his head. "That boy needs some sense drilled into his head."

I just nodded and popped one of the bar pretzels in my mouth, his comment not needing a response. He slid the drink my way and I thanked him. Before I could even ask, Benny answered my next question.

"Wish I had the first clue where he went, Ruby. You'd be the first to know, I can promise you that." He tapped the bar a couple times, making sure I caught his eyes. The sincerity was unmistakable. Benny had always been a straight shooter, and he and Carl were friendly. I knew he'd give me any info he had.

"Yeah, I know. Thanks."

I brought the straw to my mouth and Benny nodded before going to fill another order. I spun on my stool to take in the crowd. It was busy for a Thursday night. A group of bikers was shooting pool in the corner and flirting with a waitress. Another small crowd was playing a drinking game and shouting at each other while an older couple danced in front of the jukebox. I scanned the faces for one in particular, simultaneously hoping for success and failure in my quest. A second waitress wove around the tables dropping off bottles of Bud on her way back toward the bar. I gave her a small wave.

"Hey, Ruby. How's things?" Trish rested her tray on

her hip and looked me up and down. "You're looking good tonight. Hot date?"

I wanted to laugh, having asked the same question to Sadie not an hour earlier and knowing that my mission was the furthest thing from a date as possible. "Thanks, Trish. No date, just cleaned myself up a bit, I guess." I looked down at my form-fitting jeans and light blue halter tied at my waist. Rocking a bit of that retro look wasn't unusual for me, especially when I went out. It was a nice change from the Carharrts. And I was always sure to scrub my hands to within an inch of their lives—grease doesn't bother me one bit on the job, but I can't afford to buy new clothes every time I stain something.

"Well, you're cute as a damn button either way." She smiled.

"You're sweet," I told her, glancing over my shoulder to make sure Benny wasn't within earshot. "Listen. Have you seen Nash around?"

Trish's smile disappeared faster than a cold draft beer in front of Carl. Her free hand hit her hip. "Now why in the *hell* are you looking for Nash?"

I shook my head. "It's not what you think."

"It better not be." Trish flipped her bleach-blond hair and pinned me with a glare. "You've already got enough trouble, girl."

I groaned and took another sip of my Pepsi. "That's why I'm looking for Nash." Another quick glance told me Benny was still busy. He'd skin my hide if he knew I was going anywhere near Nash and his crowd. Once upon a time, I'd been a stupid seventeen-year-old looking to stir up trouble and prove what a badass I was. It hadn't taken long for me to learn my lesson and come running back from the dark side. Unfortunately, Nash hadn't been too keen on me ditching him, and it had taken the power of Carl, Benny, and Benny's favorite baseball bat to convince him otherwise. Trish had been around for a long time, so she knew the score.

"He's my best bet for finding Jason," I whisper-hissed.

She scowled at me but didn't say anything.

"I know it's a long shot, but I have to do something." I wasn't going to tell her about the garage. That was nobody's business but Carl's and mine.

"You and Carl need to learn to let that boy sink or swim on his own or he's dragging you both down with him!" Her mouth turned down and she shook her head.

"It's complicated."

Trish raised a dark eyebrow, making me wonder for the hundredth time what her natural hair color actually was. "It's always complicated, sweetheart."

My lips pursed and I waited.

She caved after about five seconds and dropped her hand from her hip. "Fine. Some of his crew were in here earlier and I might have heard something about them meeting up at Coronado's tomorrow night to watch the fight."

I leaned in and kissed her cheek, surprising her.

She pretended to shove me away. "Would you stop? It's not like I'm happy about this."

"That makes two of us. But thanks." I grinned at her and turned back to the bar. Benny wandered my way, eyeing me. Dammit. How was it that everybody seemed to be reading my mind lately? A girl likes to have her secrets now and then, for Pete's sake.

"Do I need to be worried?" Benny asked, raising a brow and setting his jaw.

Desperate to stay on his cheerful side, I put on my best smile and shook my head. "No. Now stop being so paranoid and pour me a *real* drink."

CHAPTER THREE

LEO

"Now this is more like it." Malcolm rocked the wooden bench and spread his arms out over the back with a sigh.

We both took in the view of wildflowers backed by a thick curtain of evergreens and newly leafed trees. It was springtime, and it appeared West Virginia did one hell of a job with it.

When Malcolm had balked at the idea of staying at the politician's estate, I'd suggested we try and find a bed and breakfast to let instead. That way, we'd have the security of being secluded and the authenticity Malcolm was searching for. But even Mal's giddy mood as we crossed the Shenandoah River into West Virginia couldn't lift Trevor's scowl. He and his team had been less than pleased with the new plan, and that didn't even begin to describe Alice's reaction.

But, honestly, did they really expect a rogue sniper to climb a mountain for the sole purpose of taking out two princes of little consequence? The only valid reason I could think of would involve a disgruntled boyfriend seeking revenge on Malcolm for seducing his girlfriend. Not that I had concrete evidence of such an encounter, but statistically speaking ... well.

It was true, being a member of royalty always carried certain risks to one's security, but we were four thousand miles from home. And we had the place to ourselves. It's amazing what a bit of money can do. The couple who owned the house had been only too pleased to give us free rein while they drove to the next town to visit with friends. I just hoped someone knew how to cook.

The sounds of crickets and insects I had no desire to meet created a veritable symphony around us, disturbed only by the squeak of Malcolm's rocker and the scraping of my knife on the stick I was whittling at. I admit the mountain theme was sucking me in a bit. I leaned against a nearby tree and watched as Alice emerged from the house and approached, face set in a near scowl, directed right at me. *What did I do?!*

"Sir," Alice addressed Malcolm while still piercing me with her glare. "I'd like to ask you again to reconsider." Her eyes shifted to the back of my brother's head. "As Trevor explained, they didn't have the time to survey the property and surrounding area. It's their job to keep you safe, and this current plan is making that impossible." She wrung her hands, but only I could see.

"You worry too much, Alice. Come sit and have a drink." Malcolm patted the spot on the bench next to his thigh. "We should all have a drink. Call Trevor and the boys out and we'll, I don't know, build a fire and drink Budweiser."

I stifled a laugh and Alice cleared her throat. "I don't believe that's a good idea, Sir. Alcohol impairs one's ability to react quickly."

Malcolm finally turned in his seat. "Is there something you're not telling me? Did we somehow stumble onto the mating grounds of the elusive sasquatch?" He then shot his gaze to me, eyes alight with mischief. "Now that sounds like a damn good holiday." I grinned and shaved another chunk of bark from the stick. It might come in handy should we require weapons to fight the beasts.

Alice huffed out a breath. "If you're not going to take me seriously, I'm afraid I'll have no choice but to ring the Queen."

My knife clattered to the paving bricks at the same moment Malcolm's feet hit the ground. I pushed off from the tree, whittling abandoned. "Let's not be rash, Alice. There's no need." I extended my hands.

"You wouldn't!" Malcolm challenged, his chair still and mouth agape.

My eyes met my brother's and I saw my own horror mirrored there. It was official. We'd reached the height of absurdity. We were afraid of our own mother.

Alice's chin rose. "I would. I *will*." She set her shoulders back, giving her the appearance of a mouse standing defiantly before a lion. We all knew how that story ended. "Sir," she was quick to add.

Malcolm sighed and slumped back into the bench. "Fine. Tomorrow we can stay wherever you bloody well please," he grumbled. "Even if it's a bomb shelter hidden under the bleeding White House itself if that will make you happy." He began to rock again, but with less enthusiasm than before. "But it makes no sense to relocate tonight. And besides, you haven't even started to enjoy the view." He gestured to the trees. It really was breathtaking.

Alice's expression loosened. "I'll enjoy it later. Thank you, Sir." And she turned to scamper back inside in her prim suit and heels. I watched her go, knowing like I always did, that this wasn't over by a long shot.

I sipped from the bottle of beer I'd found in the refrigerator, letting the bitter liquid pool in my mouth before swallowing. It wasn't half bad. A single porch lamp provided the only source of light as the cold metal of the car's bonnet seeped beyond the barrier of my jeans and caused chill bumps to rise on my skin. The crunch of gravel under heavy footsteps alerted me to Malcolm's presence.

"You didn't really think I'd let you get away with it, did you?"

He gasped in surprise, dropping the bag he was carrying and nearly falling backward as his hand clasped his chest. "Jesus Christ! Don't scare me like that. I thought I'd angered the sasquatches!" His voice was a forceful whisper.

The keys in his hand made a jangling sound and a laugh threatened to escape. "How in the bloody hell did you get the keys from Trevor? The man sleeps with his eyes open."

"I didn't." He gestured to the huge Suburban parked beside the BMW I was perched on. "I spiked Andrew's drink with a sedative."

I put a hand up. "Never mind. The less I know, the better. It will give me a degree of plausible deniability when you're brought before the magistrate."

He made a move toward the Suburban and I slid off the car's bonnet to cut him off. "Where do you think you're going?"

His dark brows drew together and he looked at me as if I had recently suffered a head injury. "On our road trip." He held up the keys and then snatched them away when I tried to grab them.

"Mal." The one syllable said everything I needed it to.

"Leo." His syllables spoke similarly.

We eyed each other, neither of us blinking—a practiced competition from our youth. My eyes began to sting after a spell and I had to force my lids to stay put, but I was determined to win. Malcolm clearly had the same goal in mind as his jaw clenched and blue eyes the same as mine never wavered.

One of the insects that had been serenading us all evening chose that moment to take a closer look at the inside of my eyeball, colliding with my already painful eye and causing me to slap a hand over my face. Unfortunately, I chose the same hand that held the half-empty beer bottle. It made an audible *crack* as it hit the side of my head, causing beer to foam out the top and my brother to double over in laughter.

Between his attempts to ridicule me and remain quiet in his outburst of hilarity, I barcly refrained from waking

Trevor—if only to give myself something to laugh about. But Malcolm eventually managed to calm himself. "You don't know how happy that just made me." He wiped a tear from his eye. "I win. Now go pack a bag. You're coming with me," he crowed as obnoxiously as he could while whispering.

I narrowed my good eye at him, the other one still closed as I wiped the beer from my sodden face and hair. "Neither of us is going anywhere. Trevor would shit a brick and then use it to beat you."

He waved me off. "No he won't. And, anyway, we can worry about that later." His thumb came up to rub the stubble on his chin and the delighted expression he'd worn cleared. He looked to the ground, his tone more serious—almost bordering on sullen. "This is our last chance, Leo."

He'd said *our* last chance, but I knew he meant *his* last chance. It was one thing for a prince to sow his wild oats and get into scrapes and minor scandals, but a king? It wasn't possible. It wouldn't do. He could, undoubtedly, have almost anything his heart desired—except the freedom he wanted most. This was what being born three minutes earlier than your twin bought you.

"You know they'll be packing us up in the morning and taking us back to DC—more than likely to the airport and home. You know it as well as I do." His eyes came up to meet mine—at least the one I had open. They were pleading, already colored with a hint of resignation. He stepped closer and put his hands on my shoulders. "Please, Leo. Just a few days." Then he grinned, but it wasn't genuine. "Probably not even that long. Trevor will catch up with us before we know it."

I finally opened both eyes, blinking as I focused on my brother for a long silent moment. Then I shifted my gaze to the darkened house and over to the downward slope of the long drive. Malcolm let out a breath and released his hold on me, defeat clear in both his sigh and his expression.

"If we're going to do this, we're doing it right," I said. "What are the chances we'll find some tools in that shed?"

Malcolm's eyes shot to mine and his face lit with a smile—a real one this time.

"You're like bloody McGyver!" Malcolm slapped the steering wheel with a delighted chuckle. "No, better than that. You're the love child of McGyver and Bruce fucking Wayne. If one of them were a girl, that is."

I couldn't help my smile. My skills as an amateur lock-picker and general tinkerer were proving useful on this escapade.

Once I'd made my decision to go through with Mal's plan, we didn't waste any time. I determined to buy anything I might need for the next day or so on the road in favor of re-entering the house and risking discovery. Malcolm wasn't mistaken that Trevor would find us. He'd be like a dog with a bone—a very angry dog that was likely to tear the bone to shreds when he caught up with it. But I was doing everything I could think of to at least delay the inevitable.

Malcolm took our phones to the covered porch while I poked around in the shed until I found a toolbox hiding under some garden hoses. I hauled it out and set it on the passenger-side floor of the Suburban, telling myself we were only borrowing it. Mal climbed in and started the vehicle as we both held our breath, waiting for the house to flood with light and Trevor and Alice to chase us down with scowls and pitchforks. The sound of the tires on gravel made us cringe as he turned the huge vehicle around and drove at a snail's pace in the darkness until we reached the road. Only then did we both exhale and Malcolm turned on the headlights. We shot out of there like a couple of bats out of Satan's garden.

Now that we were a few miles away, I'd opened the toolbox and was in the process of dismantling the built-in navigation system. It would do us no good to leave our phones behind while driving a vehicle that undoubtedly had tracking enabled. Malcolm's utter delight at my handiwork made me feel more lighthearted than I had in weeks. A satisfied grin settled on my face as I disconnected the last wires, leaving a gaping hole in the dashboard.

"Pull over," I directed.

Malcolm quickly complied. "Oh, please let me do the honors."

I handed the pieces over. He rolled his window down and chucked the lot out. We watched it land behind some bushes on the side of the road and I couldn't help but wince.

"I'm proud of you, Leo." He turned to me. "You've officially broken your first American law. I believe the fine for littering is five hundred dollars." His window came up again and he put the vehicle back in drive.

"Only for you. You know it goes against everything I

stand for. Oh, and I'll expect you to cover my ticket if it comes to that."

"Happy to."

We continued down the mountain in companionable silence until we reached a T in the road. Our thoughts aligning, we turned to one another and simultaneously realized the flaw in our plan. It was two o'clock in the morning on a dark mountain road in a foreign country and we had no bloody way of knowing where we were going.

Our voices synchronized just as our thoughts had and we both uttered the only word that could possibly summarize our situation.

"Balls."

Thank Christ the petrol-sucking vehicle had a mostly-full tank because it was over two hours before we finally stumbled onto the main highway and an open petrol station. We'd taken a gamble and decided to turn right at the T, both of us with a vague intuition that it would take us south. We continued making guesses until we found the station and both darted inside to collect a map and some much-needed provisions.

We'd have to spend wisely, though, to avoid using credit cards. I felt a bit like a criminal on the run from the FBI. Just call me Richard Kimble.

The attendant leaned into the counter, his head propped up with an elbow to the surface, his eyelids drooping.

"Excuse me." I cleared my throat, eliciting a slow rise of

his brows, the only indication that he was not, in fact, asleep with his eyes open. "I'm sure this will sound strange, but can you tell me where we are?"

Initially, I received no response, but then he brought himself to a more upright position and shifted his mouth to one side as he looked me over. His hair was uncombed and he wore a t-shirt that said "Blink if you like wieners." The shirt also appeared to have been made for a small child. "You mean, like, philosophically?" He scratched his exposed midsection. "Cuz that's a hard question to answer. Some might say we exist in our minds, but the 'where' can only be answered in relation to humankind as a whole. You know?"

My head tilted. "Uh, no. Actually, I meant where are we, as in, physically." I pointed both index fingers to the floor.

"Oh." He nodded. "That's a lot easier. We're at the Stop-n-Pop." Then he leaned in, getting too close for my comfort. "You got any more of whatever you've been smoking?"

I took a step back and tried to keep a polite smile. "All out, I'm afraid."

Malcolm approached, carrying several bags of what constituted a month's supply of sodium. "Are you getting anything?"

I just nodded and took another step back.

"Hello," my brother greeted the young philosopher. "You wouldn't happen to have a map, would you?"

Leaving them to it, I went in search of a bottle of water and something with a shelf life that wasn't past my own life expectancy. I was wrecked from the evening's events, and we had yet to figure out when and where we might catch some sleep. Which reminded me to grab a couple toothbrushes and some toothpaste as well. We may be living on the run, but that didn't mean we had to neglect basic hygiene.

When I brought my findings to the counter, I noticed Malcolm pulling an enormous wad of cash from his pocket. My brow quirked, and he looked from me to his hand and back again.

"You think I came up with this plan tonight? I'm disappointed you don't know me better." His head shook in mock disgust.

I merely shrugged and let him pay for our items, including a roadmap.

Out in the Suburban, Malcolm flipped on the overhead light and unfolded the map over the steering wheel while I drank from my water bottle and had a look as well.

"Here." He pointed a finger to a spot on the map. This is where we are, not far from Lynchburg. What do you say we drive to town and stop for a few hours? I could use a good kip."

Sleep had never sounded better in my life. Being a fugitive was exhausting.

After enquiring at the front desk of two hotels, we learned that it was nearly impossible to hire a room for the night without using a credit card. Since that would be the first place Trevor would look, we decided instead to find a quiet spot and sleep in the Suburban. Not the most restful slumber I'd ever gotten, but it was the only option at hand.

By seven in the morning, it was clear neither of us was getting any more sleep, so we drove to a local diner for a bite to eat. Upon hearing our accents, the waitress determined we'd be forbidden from leaving the premises without sampling their famous Virginia apple butter. Not wanting to draw more attention, we quickly agreed, having no earthly idea what apple butter might be. Given the excitement in her tone, it could be anything from a dairy product to a hand job.

"I'm going to the loo." Malcolm rose from his seat once the waitress left our table. "Don't eat all the apple concoction before I get back. If it's a local favorite, I feel compelled to try it. I'm fairly certain that's what John Denver would do."

I shifted on the vinyl seat and considered my brother. "You do know John Denver is dead, right?"

"Details." He dismissed me with a small wave and headed for the gents. I pulled out the map and studied it while he was gone. Better to familiarize myself with the area before Mal declared our next destination. Closer inspection revealed something that would likely send Malcolm into another fit. I struggled to decide if it was worth mentioning.

But I didn't get a chance to even finish my thought. Malcolm returned, his eyes wild. He pulled me up by my arm in a less than gentle manner. "Quick! They just pulled into the car park!"

There was no need to ask who he meant, but, damn, Trevor worked quickly. We must have missed something if they were able to pinpoint our location so easily. I scrambled from the booth, knowing Malcolm would just go on without me if I protested. I did manage to pull a twenty dollar note from my pocket and toss it on the table before I was being dragged down a hall and out the back door of the diner. The Suburban was parked in the front, so we had to think quickly.

"There!" Malcolm pointed to a lorry stopped at a red light on the street beside the restaurant. I didn't have time to think about how utterly ridiculous the situation was. I just followed my brother as he hoisted himself up on the long flat bed of the lorry just as it began to pull forward. Against my better judgment and my general desire to never endanger my life when at all possible, I jumped on after him and held on tight as the lorry picked up speed, taking us away from the diner, the Suburban, and all the people whose job it was to keep the future king of the Feldlands safe and accounted for.

Goddammit.

CHAPTER FOUR

RUBY

Unlike Benny's, Coronado's was a dive in every possible way. The scents of mold and smoke mingled in the air as I stepped across the threshold and into the dimly lit interior. My shoes clung to the floor with each step, making me wonder if it had ever been introduced to a mop. A white-haired older man at the bar took a drag on his cigarette and gave me a half-hearted once-over before returning his attention to his beer. The owners clearly gave no regard to the nonsmoking laws, and I wasn't about to be the one to challenge them on it. I peered around the mostly empty bar, certain that Trish had been mistaken—either that, or she'd lied to protect me. That was probably more likely.

I took a seat at the opposite end of the bar from the man and waited, hoping a bartender would appear at some point. My skin buzzed in a fire-ants-all-up-in-here way as I felt the man's eyes on me again, so I pulled my phone out in an attempt to appear busy. Never had a screensaver been so fascinating.

"If you're here for the fight, it don't start for another thirty minutes." The guy's gravelly voice carried to my end of the bar and I looked over to him before I could think better of it. "And even then, the main event ain't for a couple hours."

I gave him a polite smile and nod, hoping to God he didn't try to engage me in conversation.

No such luck.

"You know, I don't think I've seen you around here before. I think I would ..." His sentence stopped abruptly as a fit of coughing overtook him, lasting for a decent minute.

Good manners dictated that I do something—ask if he was all right or help him search for his lung on the floor at the very least. But before I could say a thing, the door to the bar opened and there was Nash, flanked by a handful of his crew.

My heart was a bongo drum and nausea swirled in my belly. I hadn't seen Nash in over a year, and that had just been in passing. My desire to punch Jason in his fat head surged again for making me purposely put myself in this asshole's path. Nash looked the same as ever, his head shaved to show off the tattoos over his ears and his body clad in his uniform of black t-shirt, black jeans, and boots. And we can't forget the chains.

This man had once defined all my teenage rebel fantasies, until I'd learned that little glamour is found in the presence of a drug-dealing, verbally abusive dickhead with an overinflated ego and an underinflated ... well, you can see where I'm going with that.

Nash spied me just as I began to have a change of heart and attempt to summon my inner David Copperfield to disappear into thin air.

"Ruby, Ruby, Ruby." He said my name as if he were sucking on a delicious candy. Ugh. So gross.

"Nash." That was all I could manage and keep from throwing up in my mouth.

He swaggered over to my barstool with a hitch in his step and a thumb to his lower lip in a series of moves I gathered I was supposed to find sexy. Instead, it had me *this* close to laughing and reminding him he wasn't, in fact, black, despite whatever little identity crisis he had going on in his head. I was reminded, once again, why he and Jason were friends.

"What brings the delectable Ruby to this part of town? I thought you were done slumming it." He grinned, and I had to admit his smile was still just as alluring as it had always been. Too bad about the rest of it.

I cleared my throat. "I was hoping to have a word with you."

"Oooh." The peanut gallery chimed in and Nash spun his head, causing them to shut up. I fought back an eye-roll as his friends shuffled forward and all took seats at a table.

The old guy, having not actually died of heart failure, rose from his stool and lifted the hinged part of the bartop, letting himself behind the bar. WTF?! He was the bartender? Good God. Without speaking to anyone, he began filling a plastic pitcher with cheap draft beer.

I turned back to Nash and caught him staring at my

rack. He didn't bother to avert his eyes before responding, "Come on. Let's go have that word in private." His hand gestured toward the door he'd just come through.

Oh, hell no! I wasn't going anywhere private with this dickweasel. Did he think I was a moron?

I shot him a strained smile, knowing I needed to at least attempt to stay on his good side. Frankly, I was lucky he was talking to me at all after the beat-down he'd gotten from Carl and Benny a few years back. I suppose time heals all wounds, and then there's always the heroin to help you forget. Pulling at my resolve, I forced my hand to rest on his arm.

"I'd rather just talk here."

His eyes took in my hand and then went back to my boobs, eventually making their way up to my face where he narrowed his gaze. "What's this about?"

I took a deep breath and let it out. "Jason."

Nash threw his head back and barked out a deafening laugh. What the hell was wrong with him?! I had no choice but to sit there patiently waiting for his amusement to subside. It took a while.

"What exactly is so funny?" I managed to keep my annoyance mostly to myself.

"Sorry, Ruby." He was still smiling and appeared the furthest thing from sorry. "I just think it's funny that you've been avoiding me for years, your nose up in the air, walking around like your shit don't stink. I mean, don't get me wrong, you're a hot piece of ass and you could do way better than this place." He gestured around the nasty bar with a finger. "But I find I'm liking it that it's your own flesh and blood that has you crawling back to me."

My hands balled into fists in my lap and I wanted to punch that smug look off his face. He knew how hard this was for me and he was milking it for all it was worth.

Being me, I couldn't keep my mouth shut. "Do I look like I'm crawling, Nash? I'm just asking a question."

He gave another chuckle. "Okay. Ask away. Just be aware, answers don't come for free."

Jesus. How had this guy not been castrated by an angry woman by this point in his life? Surely, there was a monastery out there somewhere missing its eunuch.

I swallowed hard, trying not to let my voice tremble. "Do you know where Jason is?"

His eyes ran over my face and he was silent for a beat, as if coming to some decision. Then his mouth twisted to the side and he gave one quick shake of his head. "No."

I felt myself deflate like a freaking balloon right there on that nasty barstool in that even nastier bar. Shit.

"But I may be able to find out."

My head snapped up at his words.

Nash put a hand out. "No guarantees, but I can do some asking around."

There was no doubt Nash had contacts sleazy enough to know the whereabouts of a cowardly criminal. That's why I'd come to him in the first place. But this information undoubtedly had more strings than Kim Kardashian's bikini closet (*Oh, come on—you know she has one*).

A satisfied smile crept its way across his face. Here it was. "Now. What are you gonna do for me, Ruby?" His fingers grazed the skin of my wrist and I had to suppress a shudder of revulsion.

I looked meaningfully down at his hand and then back up to meet his eyes. "Not a chance, Nash."

He huffed out a chuckle and pulled his hand back. "I figured as much. I got something else you can do for me, though."

I rose from my stool, hoping I'd have more leverage in an upright stance. "And what's that?"

Nash shot a glance to his crew and then back to me. "I've got a little issue of my own. You see, thanks to you, I'm not welcome at Benny's no more and neither is most of my crew." I had a hard time feeling bad about that so I gestured impatiently for him to get on with it. He seemed more amused than annoyed by my reaction. "I'm needing a ... presence there. One that won't raise suspicion. You get my meaning?"

Shit. I most definitely got his meaning. Well, for the most part.

"What exactly are we talking about here, Nash? I'm not dealing drugs for you so you can just get that idea out of your damn head right fucking now!"

"Calm down. Damn, girl. Not dealing. Making contacts."

My stomach rolled. I was guessing what he was suggesting was still illegal, even if it wasn't actually dealing. Dammit.

He took a step back, knowing he had me exactly where he wanted me. "Look, there's always option A."

Why was it you never had a bucket to puke in when you needed one?

I bit my lip and forced myself to picture Sadie and Carl. "Fine. What do you need me to do?"

"Where you been, Ruby? Mickey was looking for you. Said he didn't want my hands touching his baby." Carl snorted and crossed his arms.

I'd overslept—something I never do. I chose to blame it on Nash. And Jason. My night was spent tossing and turning, imagining every possible outcome of my reacquaintance with the dark side. When I'd finally fallen asleep, I dreamt that Jason and I were sharing a prison cell and Nash came to visit us. But instead of looking like Nash, he had the head of a goat. I'm sure there's some significance to that, but frankly, I didn't want to know.

I finished securing my hair into a ponytail and shook my head at Carl. "Overslept."

He narrowed his eyes. Damn the man for knowing me so well.

"No biggie, Uncle Carl. Just had a lot on my mind last night."

His suspicious look was replaced by a guilty one. We had to move things along—I didn't want him sucked into some guilt spiral.

"What's wrong with Mickey's car this time?" Mickey Hanes' "baby" was, in fact, a 1999 Ford Taurus. If ever there was a car undeserving of a pet name, it was Mickey's piece of shit car. My attempt at distraction worked as Carl's focus shifted to the vehicle parked in the second bay.

"He said it just needed a tune-up, but from the sounds it was making when he pulled up, I'd say he's about to drop his transmission in the middle of Mountain Street."

I zipped up my coveralls and grinned at Carl. "I'll have a look."

He nodded and bent over the engine of the coupe he'd been working on. We labored in companionable silence for the next couple hours. That was one of the many things I loved about working with Carl. He didn't feel the need to fill the air with pointless chatter. Aside from a few grunts elicited by tight screws and several sighs at the state of Mickey's POS, the only sounds came from the clank of tools and the faint wail of the radio.

When lunchtime rolled around, I wandered up to my apartment to throw a couple sandwiches together and grab some drinks. I brought them back down to the small office we shared and Carl practically inhaled his ham and cheese right from my hand, making me snort. I picked at mine, not really hungry.

He wiped his hands on his coveralls and swallowed his last bite. "How about I take you out for a beer at Benny's tonight? I'll even spring for a plate of nachos."

He did know my weak spots, I'd give him that. But I was supposed to go to Benny's on my first errand for Nash. I couldn't have Carl looking over my shoulder. The last thing I needed was to owe even more money—this time for Carl's bail when he killed Nash for simply breathing near me. Sweet Jesus. I'd never really thought of myself as gutter trash before, but the way things were going, I might get to wear the sash and all.

I'd never apologize for working on cars and getting my hands dirty. Or for ending the day with a bottle of Bud instead of a cosmo. But getting mixed up in the world of crime and drugs? Yeah, that wasn't something I'd be shouting from the rooftops. For the tenth time in the last week, I thanked my lucky stars that Sadie was tucked safely away at college, far from this shit. It had a way of rubbing off on you, and I'd never forgive myself if it touched Sadie.

I started as I realized Carl was still waiting for my answer, his concerned expression having returned. I needed to think fast. "Hey, why don't you let me treat *you* to dinner instead?" I could always run over to Benny's after grabbing a bite with Carl. "Maybe some carnitas at Palenque?" Carl wasn't the only one privy to weaknesses.

Despite having just stuffed his face with a sandwich, I swear I saw drool gathering at the corners of his mouth.

"Baby girl, you know I can't say no to carnitas."

That was exactly what I'd been counting on.

With a belly full of slow-roasted pork, Carl offered no protest when I dropped him off at his house following dinner. I'd been careful to only have one beer since I needed to have my wits about me at Benny's. Carl, on the other hand, took advantage of my designated driver status and helped himself to several more.

We'd talked cars and NFL draft over dinner, not that I had much stake in the latter, but I let Carl tell me all about his opinion on what he'd do if he were a team owner. Then we moved on to the topic of Sadie and her upcoming graduation. My uncle was smiling ear to freaking ear with pride and it made me want to hug the shit out of him.

He sent me one last grin before hoisting himself out of Stella's passenger seat and starting up the walk to his rental house. The place had seen better days, but I didn't think Carl had it in him to putter much in my aunt's old garden or keep up with her rose bushes. My guess was it brought back too many memories, but at least they were happy ones. Carl and Aunt Beth were still my ideal model for a healthy and happy relationship, despite her having passed three years ago. Right up until the day she died from breast cancer, Carl only had eyes for her and she for him.

My momma obviously hadn't inherited whatever genes Carl had. Pretty much as soon as I was out of diapers, she'd been more than happy to ditch me with her brother while she went off to find me a new step-daddy. The prospects she dragged back to town with her never impressed me, and vice-versa, which was how I ended up being raised almost entirely by Uncle Carl and Aunt Beth. Thank God. My induction into the gutter trash hall of fame would have occurred by my fifth birthday otherwise. At least I could be proud I'd held off for so long.

Which reminded me exactly where I needed to be at that moment. With a backward salute, Carl climbed his front porch steps and I put Stella into gear. There was no avoiding it—I was headed for Benny's and whatever shadiness I could find there.

CHAPTER FIVE

LEO

There is a reason it's illegal to ride on the open bed of a lorry. Putting aside for the moment that we didn't own said lorry, I reasoned part of the illegality stemmed from the likelihood of our bodies hurtling through the air as deadly projectiles smashing through the windshields of passing cars. I cursed my brother as the sleeve of my shirt tore in my attempt to climb toward the relative safety of the rear side of the cab. All of this while the driver remained ignorant of our presence.

Thankfully, the driver hadn't made any quick turns, as there was little to hold onto to anchor ourselves. I managed to shoot Malcolm a few glares, but my priority was staying alive long enough to punch him later. We finally came to rest at another traffic light, and without waiting to see if my brother followed, I launched myself from the lorry's bed and onto the asphalt, drawing a honk from the driver behind us. I darted to the side of the road before the light could change again and was unsurprised to find Malcolm at my side.

"That was a close one, wasn't it!?" His eyes sparkled with amusement. The enthusiasm was baffling.

"That's one way of putting it." I scowled and picked at the tear in my shirt, noting Malcolm's clothes hadn't faired any better than mine. There was a long black streak across the front of his white shirt. I took in the rest of him and noticed something else. "Where is your bag?"

He shrugged. "Left it at the restaurant. There was no time. No worries, though." He grinned. "I still have the cash so that's the important thing." He turned and started up the sidewalk as if he had a specific destination in mind.

"Malcolm!" He kept walking and I sighed in resignation before jogging to catch up with him. "Malcolm, don't you think it's time to end this little game?" I got no response, his gaze locked ahead of us. "Look, Trevor and Alice are probably ready to cut our balls off and have likely reported our antics to Mother. The longer we drag this out, the worse the consequences. We've had a little adventure and I think it's time to go back to reality."

Still nothing.

Frustration stopped me in my tracks. I couldn't follow him on this ridiculous quest of his any longer, even if it was just a stroll up the street. I'd thought we'd agreed to stop once Trevor found us. "We don't even have a car! Are you planning to walk your way across the bloody country?!" It had occurred to me briefly that we could most likely pay cash for a used car, but I didn't know how much Malcolm had on him, and there was no way he needed encouragement.

I spun around, my blood boiling, and considered walking back to the diner on my own. Screw Malcolm. But, of course, I didn't. Jaw clenched, I turned again to stare at my brother's receding back. Then with a string of filthy curses, I trudged along after him.

"You seem determined to get us killed. Why is that?" I took a bite of the energy bar Malcolm had just handed me and settled on the dusty curb beside him, legs splayed in what was either exhaustion or exasperation. I couldn't decide which. We took a break from our walk at a neighborhood shop where Mal had run in for some sustenance since we missed our diner breakfast. Now we were soaking in the mid-morning sun as we ate the granola bars, ignoring the cardboard-like texture. "Is there something I should know? Maybe a terminal illness you forgot to mention?"

He shot me a withering look and swallowed the bite he'd been chewing. "Where is your sense of adventure, Leo? I swear, keeping your head buried in your little projects has made you soft."

I barked out an incredulous laugh. "Because I don't want to hitchhike and be abducted by a serial killer? If that makes me soft, then consider me a fluffy sodding kitten."

Malcolm grunted a laugh and pushed himself to his feet. He dusted his hands on his jeans. "Don't be so bloody dramatic, my fluffy kitten. People hitchhike all the time."

My brother was clearly stuck in a 1970s movie. "Actually, I'm pretty certain it's illegal." I took another bite and forced it down. What I wouldn't give for a hot meal.

He raised a brow. "All the more reason, then. Come on." He put a hand out to help me stand and I took it. "A petrol station seems like a good place to start."

How had my life come to this? It wasn't as if I could allow the Feldlands' future king to drive off in a stranger's car with no way of contacting him. This would have to end at some point. I just needed to convince Malcolm to give in sooner rather than later. He was oblivious, whether by choice or general disregard, to the fact that our actions had consequences—and not just for us. Alice and the security team wouldn't escape this episode unscathed. Guilt clawed at me. But a glance at my brother revealed nothing but relaxed features and boyish enthusiasm.

We walked in silence until we located a station a few blocks down the road. My undershirt clung to my skin as the sun heated our backs. The scent of petrol invaded my nostrils, doing nothing to improve my mood. Malcolm immediately began to scope out the prospects while I slipped into the building, hoping he'd be too caught up in his task to notice or follow. The first thing I did was ask the attendant if they sold disposable phones. She directed me to the pharmacy next door and I slunk back out to the lot and my brother.

"I'll say one thing for the States. The sun sure shines brighter here than at home." I shielded my eyes in an overly dramatic gesture. Not that Malcolm noticed. His eyes were peeled for our potential ride and owner of the freezer that would eventually store our severed heads. "I'm going to pop over to the chemist for some sunglasses. Be right back." Not sure that he even heard me, I took off at a jog before he could protest.

A short while later, with five dollars left in one pocket and a burner phone hidden in the other, I walked back to the petrol station where Malcolm was in conversation with a tall, older bearded man standing beside an enormous black pick-up truck. They both looked up from the map my brother was holding.

Mal smiled when he caught sight of me. "Good news, Leo! He's not a serial killer!"

Several heads swiveled our way and my steps faltered, almost sending me careening onto my face and causing my brother to guffaw.

"If you boys want that ride, you better hop on in." The man nodded at me in greeting. The truck had four doors. Malcolm pulled himself up into the passenger seat, leaving me to either stay at a petrol station in the middle of Virginia or open the back door and climb in. I don't need to tell you which I chose.

Once I was settled and we pulled out of the station, I reached over the seat and handed Malcolm a pair of cheap sunglasses I'd picked up to cover my phone purchase.

"Excellent. Thanks." He then gestured to the driver. "This is Otis. He's on his way to North Carolina."

I don't know why this struck me as bad news. I suppose crossing another state line felt like we were digging our graves a little deeper. But we were already locked in and it looked like we were North Carolina bound whether I liked it or not.

I sighed and dropped my head back to the seat, but

manners dictated I at least acknowledge the favor this man was paying us. "Thank you, Otis."

He grunted in return. "Not a problem." Then he turned and inclined his head before grinning and adding, "kitten."

Otis and Malcolm howled with laughter. I shook my head and tried to cheer myself with the knowledge that I had a phone tucked in my pocket that I could use to end this at any time I chose. So I just crossed my arms and let them laugh their sodding heads off.

"I feel betrayed." Malcolm sulked in the front seat. "Of all people, I thought I could trust John Denver. He's a bloody American icon, for Christ's sake!" He threw his arms out.

"May be true, but the man couldn't read a map to save his life." Otis checked his blind spot and changed lanes, giving me a shrug of his thick shoulders in the process.

Otis had just revealed what I'd discovered at the diner earlier in the day. While our chaperoned excursion yesterday had indeed taken us across the Shenandoah River and into West Virginia, we had yet to set foot anywhere near the Blue Ridge Mountains.

Malcolm pulled out the map and spread it across his lap, undoubtedly looking for more signs he'd been led astray. His shoulders sagged.

"There's only a sliver of the Shenandoah in West Virginia anyway. Virginia and North Carolina are what that song should have been about." Otis raised a silver mug to his mouth and made a loud slurping sound. I only hoped it was coffee and not moonshine.

Malcolm's hand slapped the map. "How hard is it to pull out a map and do a little fact checking before recording an iconic song? Mountain mama, my arse!"

Otis shook his head. "What you boys need to do is take a drive on the Blue Ridge Parkway. Preferably on a motorcycle, but I'm sure it would still be worth it in a car."

Malcolm turned to him in interest. My head dropped. Otis may not be a serial killer, but putting more ideas into my brother's head was not what we needed.

"I'm dropping you outside Greensboro. All you need to do is head west and you can catch the Parkway." I didn't know what Malcolm had told Otis about our situation, but the man seemed entirely unconcerned that he was chauffeuring two foreign men with dirty clothes and no bags across state lines. I'd heard things were relaxed in the American South, but this was a new level.

Unable to do much else, and not wanting to engage Malcolm in conversation about folk hero turncoats, I rested my head against the window and closed my eyes. To my surprise, sleep overtook me almost immediately.

"Wake up, sleepy head. We're here." I felt a tap on my leg and blinked a few times, not yet fully awake. My head felt heavy as it disengaged from a dead sleep. The next thing I knew, the door I was leaning on moved and I toppled from the truck, my shoulder meeting the ground as my body rolled.

"Oh, shit," Otis said. "Sorry 'bout that."

I groaned and rolled onto my back, trying to catch my breath and get my wits about me. "No worries," I managed on a painful wince. Malcolm's face appeared over me, a hint of concern in his features, which was somewhat heartening. He put a hand out and I grabbed hold.

"Well, boys. Good luck on your trip." Otis nodded at us and returned to the driver's side of his pick-up. And then he was gone.

I looked around, having no bloody clue where we were. All I knew was I had about five new cuts and bruises and we were at another damn petrol station. If we were ever to commemorate our travels, it would take the form of a scrapbook filled with bandages and gas station receipts. It was then I remembered the phone, and my hand involuntarily darted to my pocket to make sure it hadn't broken in my fall. It seemed intact, but I'd have to examine it more closely later. As in, thirty seconds before I called Alice. Because I was calling before the day was through.

I rolled my shoulders to test my injuries. "Where are we?"

Malcolm stood with his hands on his hips and face tilted up to the sky, as if basking in the combined rays of sun and diesel fuel. His eyes were closed and I thought for a moment that he hadn't heard me. Without moving, he answered, "Kernersville, North Carolina."

I'd never heard of Kernersville, but from what our bearded friend had said earlier, I surmised it was close to Greensboro.

"So, Mal, what's the plan?" Are we hitchhiking to the mountains? Joining a biker club? Hiding out in Kernersville, North Carolina, and masquerading as bowling alley attendants for the rest of our lives?"

He finally turned to me. "We're buying a car."

Dammit all to hell.

I'd known my brother would realize this option at some point. I'd just hoped his cash was running too low to make it feasible. When I asked him how much he had, his only reply was, "Enough."

A quick inquiry at the station revealed a used car lot within a twenty-minute walk, so off we went again. I'd say one thing for this little excursion of ours—we were certainly getting our exercise.

When we arrived at the lot, I couldn't hold my laughter in at the sight of the offerings. A dozen sad heaps of metal littered the small area, each with a bright sign in its windshield touting the vehicle's winning attributes.

"100K miles and still running great!"

"1987 Buick – only one owner!"

"Water damage special!"

The owner of this lot was either running an elaborate hidden-camera scheme or was just an appalling businessperson.

Malcolm frowned at my outburst of mirth, but the mental image of him driving one of these cars was too much. His collection back home was up to a dozen cars by now, each more sporty and expensive than the last. The man would *need* to become a king in order to afford his exorbitant taste.

He marched forward in defiance and approached the first vehicle. Out of nowhere, a salesman materialized.

"This one here's a beaut! Was owned by the nicest old

lady you ever could meet. Only used the car to drive to church on Sundays. Best one on the lot!" He smiled, revealing blindingly white teeth which sat in glaring contrast to his stained polo shirt and brown trousers, which were anchored to his waist with a belt, letting his enormous gut spill over the top.

The effort it took Malcolm not to run in the other direction was both palpable and hilarious. I stood with my arms crossed, taking in the show.

"I see," Malcolm gestured to the bonnet. "May I have a look?"

The salesman's white smile faltered, but only for a split second. "Let me just go grab the keys." He turned and shuffled away. Malcolm kept his back to me, surely knowing I'd be able to see right through his expression.

"A real 'beaut,' huh, brother?" I snickered.

He mumbled something incoherent, but I did manage to make out the words "git" and "cocksucker," so I knew my comment went over well.

The salesman came walking back, breathing heavily. I had a look around from my position leaning on the water-damaged special. The view was unremarkable. Cars drifted past on the four-lane road and a half dozen fast-food restaurants lined the street along with various shops ranging from tattoo parlors and pawn shops to banks and dry cleaners. I made a mental note not to let Malcolm spot the tattoo parlor, lest he return from our trip with a likeness of John Denver tattooed on his royal arse.

A choking sound brought my attention back to the pair examining the car's engine. Malcolm wore the very same expression he'd had the moment he learned of Hugh Hefner's passing.

"I can't!" He closed his eyes. "Please shut it, for the love of God!"

Looking utterly confused and a bit concerned, the salesman did as my brother asked and shut the bonnet with a loud crash. Malcolm opened one eye at the sound, and then the other once he'd confirmed the bonnet was indeed closed.

"How could you?!" He practically shouted at the salesman before stalking off toward the sidewalk again. The salesman and I looked at one another, me with apology and he with wide eyes.

"Cheers." I nodded and followed after Malcolm. As usual. But this time I was the one smiling.

"You should have seen it," Malcolm ranted as soon as he sensed me by his side. "That man has no respect for automobiles. That engine could have been shat on by a dog, and you wouldn't have even noticed. Despicable!"

We walked a few more moments in silence. I wiped the sweat from my brow and waited for him to speak again. This would be easier if the idea to quit came from him. Two minutes turned into ten and then fifteen. I hit my threshold.

"You know what I would really love right now?"

Malcolm looked at me from the corner of his eye.

"A nice shower and a change of clothes."

"Hmm," was his only response.

Our feet kept taking us forward.

"And air conditioning," I added, again mopping the sweat from my face, this time with my torn and filthy shirt.

Malcolm finally halted. I kept going a few paces before realizing he'd stopped. I turned to face him.

"I know what you're doing, Leo."

I shrugged. "I wasn't exactly being subtle, Mal."

He shook his head and scoffed. "You can go on home if you want to, but I'm seeing this through."

I tossed my arms out. "To what end, Malcolm? You can't avoid going home forever!"

He stepped closer. "I thought you agreed we'd have this one last adventure together! Is it too much to ask to spend some time with my own damn brother?!"

I stepped closer too. "You don't seem to realize there are people whose jobs it is to keep us safe and accounted for. Not to mention people who genuinely care about our safety and wellbeing! You think Alice and Trevor, and our own bloody mother are having a grand old time?"

He waved me off. "Oh, please. They're all fine. And we're fine as well. Nobody is interested in two princes from bloody nowhere. I honestly don't even understand why we need security away from home."

It was as if he were trying to be obtuse.

"We'll have to agree to disagree on that, Malcolm. I'm calling Alice."

He laughed. "And exactly how are you going to do that?"

"We're not exactly in a technology vacuum. All it takes is a phone or a computer." Unable to help myself and no longer caring, I reached into my pocket and pulled out the burner phone.

Malcolm's jaw dropped. "Traitor!"

"Realist!" I shouted back. Then I lowered my gaze to

the phone and searched my brain for an appropriate number. Damn. I hadn't really thought about it before. I'd committed neither Alice nor Trevor's number to memory. But there *was* a number I knew by heart, having spent a childhood huddled by the receiver with Malcolm making one prank call after another.

"Thank you for calling Beckering Palace. If you know your party's extension, please dial it now." I keyed in the four-number code. "Palace Security. How may I direct your call?" A lilting female voice rang over the line.

"Good afternoon. Er, good morning?" I didn't even know what time it was back home—or here for that matter. "This is Prince Leo. It's imperative I reach Trevor Northam. I believe he's looking for Prince Malcolm and me."

"Is that so?" The lilting voice morphed into a scornful one. Shit. "Well, *Prince Leo*, if you were who you say you are, you'd have immediate access to Mr. Northam as he'd be standing beside you at this very moment." She tutted into the phone. "And for future reference, members of the royal family's phones do not come up as blocked numbers as yours has. I suggest you find other ways to waste your time. Good day." And the line went dead. Bugger!

I looked up, expecting to see Malcolm's triumphant expression, but in my complete focus on the call, I'd missed one crucial thing.

My brother was no longer in front of me, and a look up and down the street revealed he was long gone.

CHAPTER SIX

RUBY

Nothing about Benny's had changed in the last forty-eight hours, yet it felt like an entirely different place, one filled with curious eyes, undercover DEA agents, and potential crackheads hiding in every corner. I could definitely cross drug lord off my list of potential careers if the mechanic gig didn't keep me.

Benny greeted me as usual and didn't seem to find it strange that I ordered a soda again—or that I'd made an appearance twice this week. I was being paranoid.

I ran my sweaty palms over my denim shorts and gave myself an internal lecture to calm the hell down. I hadn't done anything illegal—yet.

"You doin' okay, Ruby?" Benny eyed me as he set my Pepsi on a coaster. He'd added two cherries, just the way I liked it.

I forced a smile. "Fine." Then I rolled my eyes awkwardly as I attempted a revival of bratty teenaged Ruby. It didn't work. Benny inclined his head, unamused. Luckily for me, another customer called his name from down the bar.

After a sip of my drink, I made a production of leaving my seat to take a trip to the ladies. *Nothing to see here.* A knot of guilt settled in my stomach at my act of deception toward Benny. He'd been like another uncle to me and here I was bringing potential drug activity into his place of business, his home. I pushed the thought aside, focusing on the bigger picture, on the man who was my flesh-and-blood uncle and why this was so important.

I strutted in my red platform heels to the back hallway where the bathrooms were and bypassed them entirely, heading out the exit door at the end of the hall. Outside, I found precisely what I'd anticipated. Two heads swiveled quickly my way as hands worked to disguise the joints they were holding. Never mind that the smell gave them away in a heartbeat. A trio of smokers stood to the other side, deep in conversation and minding their own business.

I made a move to approach the pot smokers, repeating the instructions Nash had given me over and over in my head. Specific words—code words. What to say and what *not* to say. Despite the cool turn of the night air, a bead of sweat ran down my spine until it was absorbed by my blouse where it tucked into my waistband. The guys looked early twenties, maybe a year or two younger than me. And suspicious. Rightly so. I was guessing I looked more likely to sell them Girl Scout cookies than smack.

I took a breath, but before I could get a word out, the

back door opened behind me and banged against the brick wall. Trish stood like freaking Wonder Woman, backlit and everything in the doorway, eyeing me like I'd just been caught stealing condoms from her purse—something I'd actually done a time or two in my wilder days.

"What are you doin' out here?" Her voice was loud and it was knowing. She turned to the duo I'd been targeting. "Get your asses out of here! You know there ain't none of that shit until we get some laws passed around here. And don't think I won't tell your girlfriend, Mitch!" she called after the pair as they darted around the building.

Her finger changed direction and pointed at me. "You get your little ass back inside, and I'd better not catch you doin' what I think you're doin' ever again. You hear me?"

My face was the picture of innocence. "I don't know what you're talking about, Trish. I just came out for some fresh air. As my words hung beside me in a speech bubble, a waft of cigarette smoke from the remaining trio formed a nicotine cloud around my head. I coughed and swatted at it with one hand while Trish grabbed my other one and pulled me inside.

Well, that hadn't gone well. I'd have zero to report to Nash in the morning, which meant he wouldn't be giving up any info he found on Jason either. I decided to wait around, hoping Trish was on the early shift and would be clocking out soon. Damn woman was too perceptive for her own good. Each time she looked at me, I graced her with an innocent smile and a wave, aggravating the shit out of her and giving me my only source of amusement for the evening.

Well, that wasn't technically true. From my perch on the barstool, I'd been texting Sadie. More specifically, drunk Sadie.

Sadie: *This guy is totally eye-fucking me from across the room.*

And by room, she meant library. Yes, my cousin was drunk in a library.

Me: *It's just like a movie. You guys can screw in the stacks. Make sure it's not some creepy section like eighteenth-century torture devices, though.*

Sadie: *You're so smart. I'll make sure I check the sections carefully.*

I chuckled to myself and took another sip of my soda.

Sadie: *Wait. What am I saying? I'm not having sex in a library!*

Me: *You know, you're allowed to have a little fun. All work and no play makes Sadie a dull girl...*

Sadie: *Did you just call me dull?!!*

She followed that with a middle finger emoji.

I loved giving Sadie a hard time.

Me: *No way. You're more fun than anyone I know.*

Sadie: *I love you so so so so much!*

I laughed out loud, drawing a glance from Benny.

"It's Sadie. She's drunk and trying to study at the library."

Benny grinned. "Tell her I say hello." Then his brows drew together and his wide mouth firmed. "And she needs someone to walk her back to her dorm. No walking alone."

He pointed at me as though I had been the one serving shots to my cousin.

"Okay, okay." I put out a placating hand.

Me: *Benny says hi and that you need an escort home. And not the eye-fucking guy!*

Sadie: *Awwww. Tell him I said hi and I love him too. I think I read the same paragraph a dozen times and it's still not making sense. Must be time for me to go.*

Me: *Get some sleep and call me tomorrow!*

Sadie: *Okay. Byeeeeeee!*

I dropped my phone to the bar, a smile plastered on my face.

The smile disappeared when I remembered my mission and the obstacles I kept encountering. Regardless of my desires, Trish was still waiting tables and it was going on eleven o'clock. Benny had hardly taken his eyes off me either, making me suspect Trish had spilled at least part of her suspicions. I bit my lip and spun in my stool to face the crowd again, Pepsi still in hand. The Wurlitzer was playing Billie Holliday's "I'll Be Seeing You," which may just be the saddest and most beautiful love song ever. It pulled at my heart every damn time. Lord knows I'd never had a guy to feel that way about, and I didn't make it particularly easy for any of them to swoon over me either. But Carl and Beth were all about that kind of love and longing, so I knew it was real.

Despite my attempts to remain positive and stay focused on working our way out of the mess Uncle Carl and I were in, I let the gravity of the whole thing sink in for a moment.

Everything I knew could be ripped out from under us

in a few short weeks. No garage, no job, no apartment. And that didn't even take into account what it would do to Carl. I closed my eyes, imagining Sadie's reaction when she was finally clued in. All her hard work would be for nothing. If I knew my cousin at all, she'd come storming back to K-ville and do whatever it took to get her dad back in business—no matter the cost to her future. A tear formed in the corner of each eye and I blinked to keep them from escaping. The last thing I needed was for Trish or Benny to see me crying, for Christ's sake.

"Can I buy you a drink?" A low voice came from beside me, making me jump in my seat.

I turned to see a guy in a blindingly pink t-shirt and drowsy eyes take the barstool next to mine. He nearly slid off the vinyl seat when he tried to overcorrect, tipping me off to his advanced level of drunkenness. Oh, goody. Just what I needed. I ignored him and looked back at the crowd, taking another pull on my straw.

"Well, if you won't take the drink, how about a fuck?"

My hand froze as I began to lower the glass. I narrowed my eyes and turned to him again. If I could get past the shirt (which I could not), the stench of alcohol (nope), and the blatant douchebaggery (hell to the no), the guy wasn't bad looking. He had wavy dark hair, a straight nose, and sculpted cheekbones. But the aforementioned details just made him an ass. And he'd picked the wrong night to tangle with me.

I spun back around in my stool and set my glass on the bar so I could give him my full attention.

"Sure. Sounds great," I deadpanned.

His brows rose and a lazy smile spread across his face.

Such a shame he was about to be roadkill under Stella's tires. He had a great smile. "Excellent. Your place or mine?" he slurred. "Oh, wait, it will have to be your place. Mine is ..." he trailed off, suddenly looking perplexed.

Jesus. This guy was wasted. His words were muddled, but it was hard to tell if it was due to an accent, excessive alcohol intake, or both.

"My place it is, then. I do have to warn you, though. I have a vicious dog who hasn't had his shots and hates assholes. Oh, and I live with my seven brothers who hate them even more. Luckily, *they've* had their shots, though." I sent him a saccharine smile and he tilted his head, clearly trying to comprehend what I'd just said.

"Hmm." He rubbed the stubble on his chin and tried leaning his elbow on the bar, only to have it slip out from under him, nearly causing his head to connect with the bartop. "Perhaps not your place, then." He paused, and I could practically hear the drunk hamster spinning the wheel in his head. His eyes found mine again, lighting a bit. "I hear motels are a terrific place for rende ... rendez ... that's quite an odd word, isn't it? It doesn't sound at all like it's spelled." He barked out a laugh. One thing was for sure —this guy was *not* from around here. I looked over the crowd to see if he'd come in alone. Somebody needed to collect this guy and take him home, and it wasn't going to be me. That was for damn sure.

I leaned into the bar to get Benny's attention.

"Good lord, your tits are fantastic," the guy said, and before I knew it, he tried to paw at my boob with a clumsy hand.

I shoved him away roughly. "Get your fucking hands off me!"

That caught Benny's attention and he was across from us in a split second. "This guy bothering you, Ruby?"

"If you call putting his hands where they most definitely are *not* wanted 'bothering,' then hell yes."

Benny's eyes drilled into the guy and he immediately put his hands up in surrender. "Sorry, but I've always been particular to large breasts." This time the foreign accent was distinct, but I couldn't quite place it. It sat somewhere between British, Scottish, and Drunkish. Whatever it was, it didn't make the pathetic apology any better.

"And *I've* always been particular to punching handsy fuckheads in the throat." Benny leaned over the bar, getting in Pink Shirt's face.

The guy didn't lean back, though. It was likely he would fall off his stool if he did. "That sounds decidedly unpleasant." He squinted.

Benny looked at me. "Who the fuck is this guy?"

I shook my head. "I have no idea. But I'm thinking he needs a cab."

My bar mate turned to me. "Wonderful! We can share. I've never been in a taxi before." His smile was leaning toward dopey.

"Not a chance in hell, buddy." I got off my stool. This night wasn't getting me anywhere. My encounter with this guy was a sign that it was time to call it a night. "What do I owe you, Benny?"

He shook his head. "On the house. Get yourself home safe. I'll take care of Romeo."

"Thanks." I waved as I stepped toward the door.

"So, does that mean no shagging tonight?" The accented voice followed me.

I didn't bother turning around. I just flipped him off over my shoulder and got the hell out of there. I'd have to figure out another way to pay my debt to Nash. But time was ticking, so I couldn't wait long.

The night had turned cool and I wished I'd brought a sweater, but I was in a hurry to get home and put an end to this day. I made it about five blocks before the chattering of my teeth threatened to break my jaw. I hated to put Stella's top up anytime after March, but tonight would be an exception. I pulled to the side of the road and secured the parking brake before climbing out and reaching for the boot covering the retractable top. As if karma was punishing me for my night's poor intentions, the damn snaps wouldn't release. It was another item to add to my Stella to-do list. I tugged carefully, not wanting to do any damage, but I could only get the first few to budge. I didn't bother to quiet my cursing and let go with a string of creative oaths.

"I can't say I've ever heard 'fuckshovel' used in a sentence before." A voice coming from way too close startled the crap out of me. I spun toward the sound on instinct, and the sudden motion caused my heel to roll under, sending me to the pavement in a heap.

"Christ! I'm so sorry!" the man said. His hand grasped my arm in a firm grip. The intrusion triggered a violent mass of emotions. Fear, annoyance, anger, pain. My face brushed the asphalt and I could feel the scrapes and cuts begin to burn on my knees and hands. I wanted to tell the stranger to take his hand off me and fuck off, but my mouth wouldn't cooperate. The emotions of the night, the week, the past month caught up with me like a swarm of bees surrounding me and sinking their stingers into my flesh all at once. There was no stopping it. I burst out into the most pathetic bout of blubbering tears in the history of girldom.

"Oh God! Did you break something?" The man's voice sounded nearly as panicked as I felt. His other hand wrapped around my side and he pulled me carefully into a seated position, relieving the grating contact of my knees with the pavement. "Shit. You're bleeding." His hands released me and I heard a tearing sound before soft cloth settled over one of my abused knees.

Entirely unable to gather myself, I continued to wail like a child, not caring that this moment of humiliation would haunt me forever. I was a ballbuster, a get-the-job-done kind of girl, not a crying kind. My hands swiped at my eyes as more tears appeared faster than I could wipe the old ones away.

I felt the stranger's ministrations on my other knee and began to shake my head. This wasn't right. I was letting some random man touch me in the middle of the street in almost total darkness. I should be running away—I should be screaming for help and calling Carl on my phone.

But his touch didn't feel threatening. It felt ... kind. Soothing. I realized then that he was murmuring a song as he tended to my wounds. I couldn't make it out, but I knew that it was not just for my benefit, but for his as well. It occurred to me then that he was a bit terrified. The thought did the impossible and allowed me to catch my breath and calm a bit.

"Oh, thank God," he said under his breath.

It struck me as an odd thing to say, until I realized his relief came from the cessation of my hysterical behavior. That made me want to laugh, but I forced the urge down, figuring the drastic switch from crying to laughing might trigger a call to a mental hospital. That would be another bill I couldn't afford.

As my eyes began to clear, I saw him sit back on his heels. He wore jeans and a torn blue button-down. My gaze rose from his shirt to his face and two thoughts hit me simultaneously. One, how had I not noticed this man had an accent? And two, I'd been followed and was probably about to die.

I opened my mouth and screamed bloody freaking murder.

CHAPTER SEVEN

LEO

Putting aside for the moment that the mere sight of my face had just made a girl scream in horror, I focused instead on getting her to quiet down before the police arrived. That would be just what I needed—police meant official reports which would undoubtedly lead to a media circus back home. I just had to find Malcolm and then Trevor and get us all the hell home.

"Please," I begged the girl. "I'm not going to hurt you. Just quiet down."

Instead of calming, though, she attempted to scramble to a standing position, only to fall again when she put weight on the ankle she'd twisted moments earlier. At least the screaming had stopped, but only in favor of more cursing at the pain of her injuries.

Her eyes flashed fire at me. "Get the fuck away from me! What is *wrong* with you?!"

I put my hands out in the universal sign for "please don't stab me." Perhaps she was drunk—or maybe in shock. "I'm only trying to help."

She laughed at that, but it was a sharp sound. "Just like you helped yourself to a feel of my boob?!"

That sent my head back. I hadn't gone anywhere near her tits, lovely as they were. I'm sorry, but I couldn't really help but notice. She wore a sleeveless top that tied behind her neck and dipped in the front. This was accompanied by some of the shortest denim shorts I'd seen in my life, revealing legs a mile long that were regrettably marred by cuts and the sad bandages I'd fashioned from my shirt.

Her face would have been beautiful, were it not set in an angry frown with drawn brows framing an intense glare aimed my way. *Revulsion.* I'd never been the recipient of that look. I imagined Malcolm had received his fair share, but the thought did little to settle me at the moment.

"I don't know what you're talking about!" I insisted. "I only touched your arm—and your waist to help you up."

She sneered at me. "I forgot how wasted you are. How did you get away from Benny?"

There was a distinct possibility she'd hit her head when she'd fallen. It was the only explanation for ...

Bloody hell!

I forced a calmness to my tone. "Remind me again, where did we meet? Sorry." I shrugged and tried for a sheepish grin. "I'm forgetful when I drink."

She just looked at me as if I were something she'd

scraped off the bottom of her shoe. Yep. She'd most definitely met my brother.

She used the door of the car to help herself to a standing position, growling angry noises my way when I extended a hand to help. Thankfully, she'd removed the red heels and tossed them into the matching red convertible. A few hobbles later and she was seated in the driver's seat, long legs hanging out the open door.

She sighed, exhaustion overtaking the annoyance in her expression. "Just go home. Please." She met my eyes, her gray ones wet and pleading. I felt a tug in my chest. "And don't follow me."

I put my hands up again, but I was beginning to panic. The moment she drove away, Malcolm's location would go with her. I needed to think fast and get her to tell me where he was. I opened my mouth to speak, but nothing came out.

She swung her legs into the vehicle and closed the door. Her hands moved to put the car in gear, but instead of the car moving forward, a high-pitched yelp erupted from her throat followed by another colorful curse. She smacked the steering wheel with her hand and then her head fell forward adding another *thump*.

She couldn't drive with her injury, that much was clear. It seemed I'd been given a reprieve. I mentally formed several explanations to volunteer, but each was likely to be met with either disbelief or possibly some form of violence. While being an identical twin is not outside the normal realm of belief, randomly running into two in one night sort of is.

She'd mentioned someone named Benny. Perhaps I could use that to my advantage. A niggling of concern for

Malcolm hit me when I remembered the girl had made it sound as if this Benny character somehow had Malcolm trapped? Restrained? Arrested? Good God.

"Can you take me back to Benny?!" I blurted before I could think better of it. This was crazy. Her head thunked against the steering wheel several times. "I mean, it's pretty clear *you* can't drive your car, but *I* could drive it."

That brought her head up. I was evidently the biggest git she'd ever met in her life by the look I got. "You really think I'm going to hand the keys to my vintage Mustang over to a guy so drunk he can't even remember where he was ten minutes ago?" A thought seemed to occur to her then and her head swung to either side, scanning the street. "Where's your car?"

I shrugged. "I don't have one."

"What do you mean you don't have one. You couldn't have appeared here out of thin air."

Another shrug. "I walked."

She narrowed her eyes at me and her lush pink lips pursed. "You walked?"

It seemed I was only capable of shrugging.

"From Benny's?"

I forced my shoulders to still. Oh. Hmm. There was no answer to this that would make sense.

"Look. I don't know what kind of game you're playing, but I left before you and you got here almost at the same time." Then her head tilted sharply to the side, more pieces coming together. "What happened to your hideous shirt?"

I looked down, fingering the torn, rumpled material. "I ripped it to make bandages." A huff of a laugh escaped me. "Well, that was part of it. The rest ... is harder to explain."

But she was shaking her head. "No. I mean, what happened to your pink t-shirt?"

I stepped back on a foot and shoved my hands in my pockets. "Oh. That."

She opened her car door and turned in her seat again, her long legs once more appearing out the side. Curiosity seemed to have overtaken her more cautious nature. "You don't know what I'm talking about, do you?"

"Um." That was all I had. But this was actually good. She was coming to the truth on her own. Maybe I wouldn't come off as a raving lunatic after all.

"And you're as sober as I am." It wasn't really a question.

I bobbed my head back and forth, considering that. "I suppose it depends. I don't know about you, but I haven't had a drop all night."

She suddenly laughed, finding something in our exchange extremely amusing. "Well, whoever you are, I can tell you your brother has had enough for the both of you."

I dropped my chin to my chest, making her laugh harder.

I pulled the car up to a brick building with neon signs in the windows and a flat rooftop. Faint music escaped the pub and drifted over the half-full parking lot. The girl called Ruby sat up a bit straighter in the passenger seat and pointed to the door as I secured the brake. "If I were you, I'd go grab him now before Benny decides to do something to him." I didn't need to be told twice.

When Ruby had realized the mistaken identity and gotten over her hilarity by the roadside, the next thing she did was hold out her hand and ask for my driver's license. Guessing—correctly—that she wouldn't know the name Leonardo Sebastian Anselm Baxter from Joe Smith, I obliged, handing her my ID from home. I was kind of at her mercy anyway, so my options were limited. I watched as she used her phone to take a photo of my ID and send it via text to someone named Sadie. I obviously had no clue who this Sadie person was, but I could only hope he or she didn't have a keen interest in geography or obscure royal families. Ruby flashed her phone at me so I could read the message.

If my body turns up in an alley, this is the guy who did it. XOXO

Then she slid over to the passenger seat and gestured for me to get in. "Nice to meet you, Leonardo. I'm Ruby." She shot me a wide smile that nearly sent me tumbling out the open door. Her makeup was smudged and her eyes tired, but her smile—it was brilliant. I barely managed to steady myself and act like a normal human long enough to shut the door and fasten my seatbelt.

"Let's go get your drunk-ass brother."

I couldn't help but smile in return. "You didn't even ask if I know how to drive."

She shrugged. "Desperate times and all that. Besides, I'm not sure how long your brother has to live if he decides to hit on one of the waitresses."

That got me pressing the gas. If Malcolm died, I'd have to take his place, and I had other plans. Besides, King Leo just didn't have that ring to it.

"Are you from the UK?"

"Around there, yeah." I couldn't have her looking the Feldlands up on the internet and outing us. Partial truths would have to do.

She seemed to accept my answer and directed me to a neon sign on the left as I snuck glances at her legs.

As it turned out, Benny's Bar was only a few blocks away and I hadn't been far from Malcolm at all. Considering we'd both been on foot for the evening, I suppose it wasn't that surprising.

I pushed open the door and scanned the dimly-lit interior. Billiard tables lined one wall and a long bar lined the other. In between were scattered tables and vinyl-trimmed chairs, most of them occupied. I did a double take when I caught sight of an enormous mounted animal head above the bar. It looked like ... a wooly mammoth. That was ... odd, to say the least. But my attention didn't remain there long. A voice I knew as well as my own rang out above the din. "Would I lie to you?! I swear it on my mother's grave!"

Malcolm stood wearing a neon pink t-shirt, his shoulder leaning into the wall and his back to me. I now understood Ruby's reference to the hideous shirt. In front of him stood two large men in black leather vests, kerchiefs tied around their heads and expressions that could only be described as tolerant. I moved in immediately.

"Although that's not saying much, I admit. The old bat is still alive and well, but all signs point to her being a vampire, so the grave part could be valid."

"Malcolm," I said as I reached his side. He turned and steadied himself with a hand to the wall. I instinctively reached out and grabbed his arm to help.

"Leo!" His grin was lazy and his voice booming. He came in for a back-pounding hug and I shook my head as he draped his pickled body over me. "Boys! This is my brother, Leo. The one who replaced all the photos in the palace with pictures of Willem Dafoe. Scared the absolute shite out of Father, didn't you?"

It was worse than I feared. Malcolm was at the reminiscing state of intoxication. He'd also forgotten he was angry with me—and that we were trying to keep a low profile. He pulled back to look at me and clearly had trouble focusing. With a pat to my shoulder, he asked, "Will you buy me a drink? The bartender refuses to serve me."

"Come on. I've got drinks outside." I gestured to the door and then nodded to the two men, making certain to shoot them a look meant to say, "Ignore this drunk git who's definitely *not* a prince." One of them wished me luck and they both turned for the pool tables.

"We'll talk again tomorrow!" Malcolm shouted after them. Then to me, he stage-whispered, "I think they're part of an outlaw biker gang."

"Ah," was my only answer. Leave it to my brother to create drama where there was none.

I led him toward the door. A muscular bald man in a black t-shirt signaled to me from behind the bar. "You got him?"

I gave a thumbs-up and opened the door for my mess of a brother. Even before I could lead him in the direction of Ruby's car, he choked on a gasp. "Sweet Jesus! Am I dead?" His eyes homed in on the classic red convertible and the gorgeous girl in the passenger seat. Never mind her eyes had him in a tractor beam of disgust. He darted a glance my way.

"Not yet. But it's still early."

We approached, me supporting a good portion of Malcolm's weight, and Ruby pointed a threatening finger at him. "Rule number one: Every part of you stays in the backseat. If you so much as place a finger in the front, I won't hesitate to throw your ass on the sidewalk."

Malcolm stopped in his tracks, causing me to almost knock both of us over. One glance told me he was absorbing Ruby's words. He nodded and took another step.

"Rule number two: Keep your mouth shut. I don't need to hear anything else you have to say tonight."

Malcolm's steps halted again. He seemed unable to use his ears and legs at the same time. I released a sigh of frustration and dragged him the rest of the way, shoving him into the back seat before settling in the driver's seat.

"You tricky bastard! You—" he began, but Ruby cut him off with a quick "Nope!"

I turned and watched him mime zipping his lips as he shot me a look that was equal parts anger, amusement, and awe. I didn't bother to correct him on any assumptions he was making. My eyes fell to his t-shirt and I felt my lips curve in a disbelieving grin. Not only was it bright pink, but it had a logo emblazoned on the front featuring a mouse and the words "Save a Mouse. Eat a Pussy."

"Where in God's name did you get that t-shirt?" It certainly wasn't what he'd been wearing earlier.

He shook his head and pointed at his mouth.

Ruby muttered, "Damn straight," as I put the car in

reverse and backed out of our spot, unable to suppress my smile.

"So," Ruby began. "Are you going to tell me how you ended up wandering down Main Street in Kernersville, North Carolina, with that accent, those clothes, and no car?" She pointed to the right, directing me.

I cleared my throat and pulled out onto the street. "It's, uh, complicated."

"Ah. Now that's something I'm *very* familiar with." I glanced her way and found her examining her knees with a wince.

"You need to clean those wounds before you get an infection." I nodded at her legs, grateful for the excuse to check them out again. All that creamy skin—it seemed a crime she might develop scars.

She smoothed the makeshift bandages back in place and shrugged. "I will when I get home." She bit her lip then. "Thanks for driving me, by the way. I'll be happy to pay for an Uber to get you wherever you're staying." She shot me a glance. "Within reason, that is." A grin formed on her delectable mouth. Now that she was reserving her acidic expressions for Malcolm, I was able to take in precisely how lovely her face was. Big gray eyes framed by thick lashes perfectly complimented her generous mouth and freckled nose. Most of her makeup had smeared off during her crying jag earlier, and there were black smudges under her eyes, but I barely noticed. I swallowed hard and returned my focus to the road.

Ruby directed me through a few turns, finally instructing me to park in front of an auto shop. The sign wasn't lit, but I could still make out the name. Crankshaft

Auto Repair. I looked at her in silent question, then glanced around for a sign of a house. Nothing—just a tobacco shop and a laundrette flanked the garage. I pulled in and parked, as instructed.

"We're at the right place. Don't worry." We both opened our doors, and I rushed around to help her, but she declined my hand with an appreciative smile. Malcolm was —shockingly—still silent. However, a glance to the back seat showed him sprawled with his head back, mouth open, and consciousness long gone. He'd passed out drunk in the back of Ruby's car.

"Shit."

Ruby followed my gaze at the expletive.

"Shit," she echoed.

We both looked around, me still wondering what we were doing here and Ruby lost in her own thoughts. She inhaled deeply and squinted as she pondered the situation.

I just scratched the back of my neck. It was one thing helping my brother out of a car, but another dragging his unconscious carcass out. And where would we go, anyway? I made a note to go through Malcolm's pockets as soon as bloody possible so I could at least get the cash which he, hopefully, hadn't blown on anything foolish in the hours we'd been apart. It was clear from the t-shirt and the alcohol he'd been marinating in that his judgment wasn't unquestionable.

Ruby let out the breath she'd been holding and leaned into the car door for more support. "Okay. There's no way an Uber driver is going to let *that*,"—she pointed to Malcolm—"in their car." I nodded and she continued, "Where are you staying anyway?"

I went for my second sheepish grin of the evening, hoping it held at least a little charm. More than likely, it just looked pathetic. "Uh, I hadn't quite figured that out yet."

Her brows almost hit her hairline. "You weren't kidding when you said it was complicated." Her eyes narrowed then, making me want to smile at how expressive her face was. "You're not running from the law or something, are you?"

I laughed at that and shook my head. "I promise you, we're not that exciting." I weighed how much to share. "We're actually just on a short road trip gone wrong."

She examined me, evidently looking for signs of criminal intent—or lasciviousness. Then she nodded and hooked a thumb toward the auto shop. "All right, here's the deal. I live above the garage. There's a couch in the office downstairs. It's not the most comfortable thing in the world, but it's better than sleeping outside. We'll pull Stella into one of the bays and let your brother work on his oncoming hangover, and you can stay in the office."

My eyes went wide. "This is *your* shop?"

Her hand went to her hip. "Care to take that surprised look off your face? Yes, it's mine. Well, mine and my uncle's."

I winced, knowing I'd cocked that up. But I didn't think I'd ever met a female mechanic. Which was even more blatantly sexist, I realized. How many mechanics—man *or* woman—did I actually know? I decided a plain, "Thank you," was the best response. My wince-face remained in place, however as I raised a hesitant finger. "Just one question, if I may. What or who is Stella?"

I got a look I'm reasonably sure Malcolm had experienced several times already from Ruby. "Uh, the Mustang." The implied "you git" was left off the end of the response, as was the finger flick to the forehead.

But I wasn't about to protest. I was, in fact, an utter git at the moment. The important part was we had a place to crash for the night, and tomorrow I'd get hold of Trevor if it killed me.

CHAPTER EIGHT

RUBY

I must have had a screw knocked loose when I fell earlier. There was no other explanation for why I was letting two complete strangers stay in the garage overnight. Carl would rip me a new one for that, so it was a good thing tomorrow was Sunday and the garage would be closed. Not that these guys were particularly intimidating, mind you. I was pretty sure I could take brother number one, especially given his current state. And, in fact, Leonardo was almost painfully polite—apart from his clear surprise at the thought of a delicate flower like me knowing a thing or two about cars.

The accent didn't hurt either. He'd said they were from "around" the UK, whatever that meant, and it made sense in terms of the accent, although they seemed to borrow a bit of tone and vocabulary from the U.S. too. Unlike his brother with the slurring, cocky overtones coloring his voice, Leonardo's accent was crisp. And, I must admit, kind of did something for me. What a freaking cliché I was. This was exactly the kind of behavior I rolled my eyes over when other women did this shit.

Never mind. It wouldn't be an issue because the Baxter brothers would probably be gone before I even came downstairs in the morning. So there was really no harm in looking, was there? The brothers were identical, so I'd already had the chance to take in the cheekbones and the smile, but I was allowed to actually enjoy them on Leonardo. After all, he hadn't propositioned me and attempted to grope me in the middle of a bar. So enjoy I did. His hair was so thick it was begging me to reach out for just a tiny touch. Why was it guys like him got better hair than girls? Not that I hated my hair or anything, but I wouldn't say no to borrowing a bit of his volume.

Okay. That was enough.

In my bare feet, I hobbled over to the glass door, pulling my garage key from my purse and feeling every little rock and pebble under my soles. My ankle was throbbing, and trying to walk on it was only going to make it swell up like a balloon. Leonardo tried to help me but I waved him off. I was already admiring his looks and manner too much. The last thing I needed was for him to make physical contact.

Once I opened one of the bay doors, he pulled Stella in and carefully parked her before getting out and heading my way again. He stopped mid-step, though, and reached into the passenger seat to retrieve my patent-leather platforms. They were almost as pretty as Stella. He examined them as he approached me.

"Honestly, I'm shocked you haven't already broken something wearing these things. They're ridiculous." His mouth quirked.

I reached out and snatched the shoes from him. "They're fabulous!" My scowl bounced right off him. "And besides, *Leonardo*, you and pussy boy over there are the last people I'd take fashion advice from. I gestured up and down his bedraggled form and then to his brother in that awful shirt.

He scowled back at me. "Point taken. But it's *Leo*, not Leonardo."

Leo.

Yeah, that was better. It suited him.

I forgot about my ankle for a minute and smiled at him. He smiled back. We stood there like two idiots, forming our own goddamn mutual admiration society. Something about the way I was looking at him made his smile grow, giving me a glimpse of his straight white teeth and putting deep parentheses on either side of his very kissable mouth. I tried to keep from looking at it, but it was no use, and before I could stop myself, my tongue slipped out and wet my lower lip.

He made some kind of sound and my eyes shot up to his. In the minimal light of the garage, I could tell his eyes were blue, but what captured my attention were his pupils. I'd seen pupils that size before, and it could only mean one thing. I was guessing if I looked south, I'd see something else that was larger than usual. The horny part of my brain was ready to take a closer look and see what we were working with. But cooler heads prevailed.

Leo and I both seemed to snap out of it at the same

time. He took a step back and ran a self-conscious hand through his hair. This didn't help. It only reminded me that I hadn't gotten to touch his hair yet—nor would I ever. This had to stop now.

I cleared my throat and motioned to the office door, certain I looked as awkward as I felt. "The couch is in there. If you wouldn't mind, can you close the bay and lock the door?" I gestured to my ankle as an excuse, but I just needed to get out of there before I did something stupid. I took a hesitant step toward the stairs, using Stella to support me.

His brows drew together. "How are you going to get up those stairs?

I hadn't really thought of that, but I waved him off. That only made his eyes narrow. Wherever he was from, they either took manners very seriously or had a population of helpless women.

"Look. I know you don't know me from Adam, but I can certainly help you up the stairs without violating any codes or personal boundaries. It will be easier." He took a step closer, making the hairs on my arms stand up straight. If this boy touched me, I could not be responsible for my actions.

I quickly shook my head and half limped-half hopped to the foot of the stairs before he could protest again. Without looking back, I said, "Good night, Leo. It was nice to meet you." And then I pulled myself up the stairs one painful step at a time, driven by the knowledge that a cold ice pack and a warm bed awaited me. I had too much on my plate to risk distraction from a cute boy who flipped my switches.

Miranda Lambert's "Fastest Girl in Town" startled me awake in the too-early hours of morning. I hadn't fallen asleep until half-past two from the discomfort of my ankle and the unsettled feeling I had knowing the Baxter brothers —two complete strangers, I had to remind myself—were just downstairs from me. Not that I thought they'd do anything. I was just intensely ... aware. One look at my phone told me two things I already knew. It was freakin' early, and Sadie was about to be all up in my business.

"You'd better be calling me this early to tell me you got laid by Charlie Hunnam or Kit Harington." My voice sounded like I'd swallowed a porcupine.

"Please, woman. Kit is too short for me. Charlie, on the other hand ..." She was way too perky for someone who was library drunk not eight hours earlier.

"Out with it. I'm operating on less than four hours of sleep here." Sadie was used to my morning mood.

"Me? How about you?! I just saw your text from last night. Who in the hell is Leonardo Baxter? And please tell me he's in bed next to you." She cackled, making me pull the phone from my ear. I needed coffee.

"It's a long story, and I hate to disappoint you, but he's not in my bed." I rolled over onto my back, running a hand through my mess of hair. I hadn't even bothered to brush it out last night when I'd come upstairs. I had, however, stared at the mirror in horror over the state of my mascara-streaked face and the knowledge that I'd been mooning over this Leo guy while looking like Lindsay Lohan preparing for her mugshot. It was not a good look.

"Is he on a coffee run, then?" Sadie's voice was hopeful.

I coughed out a laugh. "No, Sadie." And then, it must have been the sleep deprivation that caused me to continue. "He's sleeping on the office couch."

She inhaled sharply. "No way!" There was a shuffling noise as she switched the phone to speaker. "Hold on, I'm taking another look. Oh my, he's super hot if his ID is anything to go by. Where the hell is Dunwall anyway?"

"Not in the U.S., that's for sure." And again with the case of verbal diarrhea, "He has an accent." I wanted to elbow myself violently in the face. Why did I have to tell her that?

She sighed. "Is it super sexy? I'll bet it is or you wouldn't have mentioned it. Oh my God. Do you have a crush on this guy?"

"What?! No! Jesus, Sadie. He just needed a place to crash."

"And you let a complete stranger who just happens to have a sexy accent and *that* face sleep in the same office you won't let Jason even set foot in?"

I pulled my hand from my hair. "To be fair, Jason is a known criminal. And I felt bad for the guy. His brother was passed out in Stella's backseat." I actually clapped a hand over my own mouth at that overshare.

"Brother?! You are not getting off this phone until I have the whole story, Ruby. I hope you know that!"

I sighed and pulled my covers off. The sight of my bandaged knees and swollen ankle gave me pause and I noticed new tinges of purple appearing on the skin. Dammit. "Give me a minute. I need coffee." I gingerly swung my legs to the side, hesitating to attempt rising from the bed. I told myself to man up and grabbed onto the bedside table for support. As soon as my bad foot tried to take any significant weight, a shooting pain ran up my leg. "Ow! Shit!" I sucked in a breath and steadied myself.

"Ruby?! What's wrong?!"

I swore again. "Nothing. I hurt my ankle last night, and I just put too much weight on it, that's all." I managed a small hop toward the kitchen.

"It sounds bad, girl. Have you seen a doctor?"

I tried to reign in my sarcasm but it was no use. "Sure. Right after I paid my country-club dues." I immediately felt bad, so I calmed my tone. "Sorry. It's fine. Really. I just twisted it. Some ice and ibuprofen and I'll be good as new."

"Do you need me to come home, Rubes? I don't have class till tomorrow." I could hear her shuffling around her room, probably packing a bag already.

I was shaking my head even before she finished. "No way. I'm completely fine." She'd find out about Jason and our huge mess if she so much as set foot in K-ville. She was staying in the mountains where she belonged—kind of like that Heidi chick. A mental image of Sadie in a milkmaid dress, her long blond hair in braids, made me smile. All she needed was a cow. Or was it a goat? Whatever. I was about to drive home the point that she shouldn't come home when there was a knock on my door.

Shit. It could only be one of two people, and I was guessing the second one had his head buried in the toilet bowl downstairs right about now.

"Sadie, I know you're going to kill me, but I have to call you back."

"What?! No! No fair. What's going on?"

"I believe Mr. Baxter of Dunwall is at my door."

She squealed and I immediately hung up on her.

I dropped my phone on the couch and managed to hop on one foot to the door, stopping along the way to balance myself on a dining chair or two. Being a cripple worked up a sweat. "Just a second!" I called out so he wouldn't think I was dead.

After releasing the lock, I opened the door to find Leo, now dressed in just a white t-shirt and jeans, standing on my doorstep. His dark hair stuck up on one side and his face needed a shave—or not. Suffice it to say, morning looked good on him. It could have been my imagination, but I believe my thighs began to tingle.

"Hey," I managed to say, my voice only cracking a little.

I got no response. It was then I noticed his eyes were not on my face but a bit farther south. I followed the direction of his gaze and, lo and behold, I was still in my freaking pajamas. And by pajamas, I mean a tank without a bra and a pair of knitted short, short, *short* shorts. Well, shit! I immediately crossed my arms over my chest, removing my only means of support keeping me upright since my hand was no longer holding onto the door frame. "Shit!" I started to fall sideways and abandoned all modesty, gripping onto both my entry table and Leo's arm and letting my boobs fly about as they pleased.

"I got you." Both of Leo's hands gripped me and pulled me back to an upright position, putting us in close proximity. There were so many things I wanted to cover—my boobs, my crotch, my morning breath, my entire head with a paper bag. But I let him steady me and even tried for a hint of a thank you smile. "I didn't mean to bug you, but I heard you yell from downstairs and I wanted to make sure you were okay." His eyes moved to my ankle where it looked as if my foot had swallowed a softball and deeply regretted it. "I see it's still bad. Did you ice it?"

I nodded, not wanting to speak and kill him with my dragon breath. I started to turn and he kept hold of me as I moved us toward my kitchen table where I collapsed in a chair and resumed hiding my tatas. "I iced it last night, but I'll do it again."

Leo, ever the gentleman, motioned to the freezer and I nodded. "Sure. Thanks. There's an ice pack in the door." I was proud my voice sounded so normal. He moved to the freezer and my eyes very innocently swept up and down the back of him. It had been dark last night, so I hadn't gotten the full effect. His t-shirt was untucked and his jeans rode low on his hips, making me think it was a good thing he had a firm ass or those jeans would be in a puddle at his feet. Or, wait, was that a good thing? Ummm. I leaned into the table and rubbed my hands over my face.

"How's your brother feeling this morning?" I forced out.

Leo opened the freezer and examined the door's contents. "Not sure. He was still asleep when I came up here. I imagine regret will be among the first of his feelings, though."

I grinned at that and Leo brought the frosted blue gel pack over to the table. "You never told me his name."

He handed the ice pack over and sat across from me, tilting his head curiously. "I would have thought he'd told you that himself. Maybe it's outdated thinking, but I believe it's customary to introduce yourself before molesting a beautiful woman." A hint of pink touched his cheeks as he seemed to realize he'd just called me beautiful. Well, wasn't that just the sweetest thing? I couldn't even decide which I liked better, the compliment or the blush.

I pretended not to notice either and laughed. "Well, he obviously hasn't read the latest Emily Post book." I grabbed the ice pack and maneuvered myself into a position where it could rest on my ankle and I could retain what little modesty I had left.

"Malcolm. He's called Malcolm. Or Mal." He chuckled. "Or cocky bastard depending on who you ask."

"I think that's the one I'll use."

"Well, I'll be happy to hold the cocky bastard down while you punch him. He clearly deserves it." His fingers traced a scratch on my table.

My ice pack slid and I readjusted it. "You mean you wouldn't offer to punch him for me?"

"I'd be happy to." His fingers continued their glide along the painted surface, and there must have been something seriously wrong with me because I felt my nipples tighten under my tank. Thank God my arms were shielding them from view. "I'm just respecting your right to first dibs. And, besides, I haven't missed that you like to fight your own battles."

I smiled at that. Who *was* this guy?

Leo leaned in closer and I involuntarily did the same. "And between you and me," he stage-whispered, "you probably have a better right hook."

Oh, I liked this guy. He was full of shit, but I liked him. He could stroke my ... ego ... any time he wanted.

The pack slid again and I bent to move it. Leo eyed my awkward position and his mouth turned down. "Hey, I want to apologize again for giving you a fright and making you fall last night."

Giving me a fright. Oh, wow. That was damn near irresistible. But I waved off his concern. I'd hurt myself way worse than this doing stupid shit over the last twenty-five years.

He moved to stand again. "It hurts looking at you all contorted like that. Why don't you settle on the couch and prop your foot up?"

I started to shake my head, thinking it would probably just be best if he saw himself out and got back on his way. This had been an amazingly enjoyable distraction, but I had plans to make and losers to hunt down. My protest died on my tongue at his next words, though.

"I saw a bakery just down the block. I can run and grab coffee."

Damn my addiction.

"And maybe some pastries?"

Strike that. Damn my addictions.

I sighed and adopted a put-upon expression. "If you must. I suppose I could tolerate some coffee."

He grinned, causing his eyes to practically freaking sparkle.

"And a cherry Danish," I added.

His grin grew.

"Or peach if they don't have cherry."

He nodded, still with the eye sparkle.

"But under no circumstances should you get apple. If that's all they have, a donut with chocolate frosting and sprinkles will do."

"Got it." He held out a hand to help me up and I took it. "Coffee and cherry Danish. Peach is acceptable, but apple is offensive and possibly criminal. And the donut thing if all else fails."

I nodded and rose to standing, finding myself within only a few inches of his face. I forgot about my morning breath and my high beams. The blue of his eyes was rimmed with a color so dark it almost matched his pupils, which were not as large as they'd been the night before, but they had potential. Flecks of navy peppered his irises, making them come alive. My gaze volleyed back and forth between his eyes and then, without my permission, fell to his mouth. Just as mine had last time, the tip of his tongue swept across part of his full lower lip before disappearing back into his mouth. I used the tiny sliver of restraint I still held to keep myself from leaning in and taking that bottom lip between mine. I forced myself to speak instead.

"I like my coffee with lots of cream and sugar." My voice came out all winded, like I'd just finished hot yoga or something.

If I hadn't been so close I wouldn't have noticed the slight quirk of his lips at that. This man was clearly some kind of wizard, using his fancy wizardy shit to reel me into his sexy zone. I broke eye contact with any part of his face and turned my head toward the couch. My movement seemed to sever the connection on his end as well, and he cleared his throat before helping me to the couch and leaving the apartment with a quick, "Be right back."

As soon as the latch clicked in place, I yanked the throw pillow from behind my head and held it over my face, screaming into it and trying to erase the last ten minutes from recorded time. Instead, my brain chose to tattoo it to the inside of my skull for easy access if I ever needed to replay it.

CHAPTER NINE

LEO

"Wake up, douchebag!" I wasn't gentle in my rousing attempts. Malcolm groaned and snuffled, eyes still closed. "Mal, you've got to get up." I shoved his shoulder again, causing him to tip over in the seat. His head made contact with the door.

"Ow! What? Ow." His hand rubbed at his temple while he blinked his eyes open and let out a pained groan, this one lasting a full ten seconds or so. It seemed the hangover was finally making itself at home.

"I thought about making your coffee Irish, but figured good old black was more suitable." I set the cardboard cup on the boot of the convertible—Stella. The thought of Ruby naming her car made me want to smile. The thought of Ruby herself made me want to do other things. Lots of things.

When she'd answered her door in that thin cotton top with the barely-there shorts, I lost my ability to speak. I stared at her breasts like a pervy old man, and I knew she caught me before I got control over myself. It had been all could do not to barricade myself in the apartment with her and tell her all the reasons having a one-day fuckathon would be in everyone's best interest. There was no denying it—Ruby was temptation itself. But she was also a diversion I couldn't justify.

I was reminded of this as I took in Malcolm's pathetic pink form sprawled across the convertible's backseat, his head in his hands and his moans of pain and regret filling the lonely garage.

"Good lord," he finally said. "What happened last night?" He lifted his head, squinting as he looked around. "And where in the bloody hell are we?"

"I'll explain later. For right now, you need to drink that coffee and try to clean yourself up. There's a bathroom in the office." I pointed toward the open door a few yards away, then made a move to the stairs, a drink carrier and bag of pastries in hand.

"Where are you going?"

I didn't bother looking back. "None of your business."

Malcolm sputtered behind me, but my steps didn't slow one bit. I practically jogged up the stairs. At the top, I knocked and then let myself in, not wanting Ruby to try getting up again. She was just where I'd left her, looking sleep-rumpled, half-naked, and unbelievably hot. Her hair splayed out in a riot of long gold and bronze waves around her, making me imagine it draped over my skin. The effort it had taken to cool myself off on the way to the bakery was all but wasted at the sight of her.

There was, however, one saving grace. I had to work hard not to laugh at the throw pillow resting on her chest. Not that it wasn't a wise idea on her part—and kind of a relief to me, if I were being honest. The temptation to take in her gorgeous tits in that nearly sheer top was a true struggle. I'm only a man, after all.

Her eyes lit as I approached, and my ego sat up a bit straighter, until I noticed they were focused on the treats I'd brought.

"Coffee with cream and sugar for the lady." I held out the large cardboard cup and she adjusted carefully to a more upright position before grabbing it with two hands in an almost predatory manner. Mental note: don't come between Ruby and coffee.

Then I extended the white bakery bag. "I got you a few things."

She peered at it but didn't let go of her coffee to take it from me. I opened the bag and held it out for her to peek inside, prompting a smile. "Oh my God. You got a bear claw! Why didn't I think of that?"

I'd actually bought more than just a bear claw, whatever that was. When faced with the overwhelming number of choices, I selected the requested cherry Danish and then asked the server to fill the bag with an assortment of other treats. I didn't know what half of them were, but they all seemed to contain the crucial ingredients of butter, flour, and sugar, so I figured I was good.

"Oh, and is that a pecan roll?" Her eyes rose to mine. "You are seriously good at breakfast."

I coughed out a laugh, finding her definition of breakfast to be not only amusing but a bit worrying. I set the bag on the side table and took my own coffee before abandoning the tray. I motioned to the chair across from the couch and Ruby shook her head and smiled. "Sorry! Of course. Have a seat. And thanks for the coffee." She raised her cup in a toast before taking a careful sip and sighing.

The coffee was decent, I had to admit, but I liked watching her enjoy it more.

"So, I'm guessing you're heading out after this?"

Was that disappointment in her voice?

Great, now I was projecting. Malcolm's flair for drama was becoming contagious.

"Yes. I've been trying to find our ride," I simplified my response, pulling the phone from my back pocket and looking at the still-blank screen. My call to security last night had resulted in a similar response to the first one, although at least I was able to leave my number this time. I was beginning to think I'd need to call my mother, and nobody wanted that. My true hope was that she remained blissfully ignorant of our disappearance—although the blissful part was unlikely. But the fact that the security office still seemed to think Trevor was with us led me to have some hope. Heads—and balls—would roll once Mother found out.

Since Trevor hadn't magically appeared overnight and taken over the auto shop SWAT-team style, I had to assume whatever tracking device he'd used to trace us to Lynchburg must have been in either the Suburban or Malcolm's abandoned bag. Which reminded me that I now had several thousand dollars resting in the pocket of my dirty jeans. Malcolm would be predictably livid when he discovered I'd picked his pockets.

"So, you want to tell me your story while we wait?" Ruby coaxed.

She oozed curiosity and devilishness, which made it impossible to deny her. And there wasn't any reason not to share the vague details, so I did.

"We were supposed to be in the States to attend ... meetings for a week. In D.C." That wasn't a lie. "But Malcolm got the bright idea to add a side trip to our schedule—a pilgrimage of sorts dedicated to that song about West Virginia. You know, the John Denver one."

She nodded, finally setting her coffee down and pulling the bakery bag onto her lap. "Of course. Everybody knows that song." I admit I was surprised at her casual acceptance of the notion that two grown men would embark on such an odd journey. Maybe it was an American thing. She pulled out the pecan roll and inspected it before replacing it in the bag and taking out a glazed monstrosity and eying it like prey. "So why aren't you in West Virginia?" She took a huge bite and moaned.

I lost my mind for a moment and had to reposition myself in the chair and turn my thoughts to war and football. After a breath, I shook my head and took another sip of coffee. "That would take too long to explain, but suffice it to say, we took a detour and kind of ... um ... lost our vehicle."

She lowered the pastry to her lap, her eyes wide and her mouth turned down. "How in the hell do you lose a car?" I had the distinct feeling that had Stella been within reaching distance of the couch, Ruby would have stroked her like a beloved child, telling her not to listen to the mean man.

I scrambled to amend my statement. "We know where it is, we just don't have it anymore." I sighed when her expression didn't change. "Okay. There were other people on the trip with us. They wanted to call it quits and go home. Malcolm wanted to continue. And he's my brother." I shrugged. "So we ditched them."

Her face lit and she laughed. I felt like I'd just been awarded a trophy. Best Non-Asshole goes to Leo Baxter. "Good for you! So, where are you headed now?"

It was my turn to frown. As ridiculous as it was, I didn't want to disappoint her and tell her I was trying to get us home as soon as humanly possible. But she couldn't understand the underlying issues without me divulging our true identities. I was considering outright lying—it wasn't as if I'd see her again, so what was the harm, really? But before I could say a word, another voice startled the hell out of both of us.

"We're going to drive the Blue Ridge Parkway."

Ruby stood, the contents of her lap hitting the floor as her ankle once again protested and she let out a curse before falling back to the couch. "Haven't you ever heard of knocking?!" she yelled at my brother.

I shot him a frown, but he ignored it, strolling into the room, coffee cup in hand, awful shirt still adorning his chest.

"My deepest apologies." He gave a mock bow. "I did knock. I suppose you were too engrossed in your conversation to notice." His gaze traveled back and forth between us before his eyes narrowed on me and his lips turned up. Shit.

Ruby's frown matched my own as she repositioned herself and then stared down at the mess of pastries on the rug. "You owe me a bear claw," she growled at Malcolm.

He just nodded and continued to grin at me. How was he still functioning after the amount of alcohol he'd consumed? "I'll be more than happy to provide the lady with *whatever* she desires—be it bear or man." He shifted his gaze to Ruby and winked.

She just turned to me in response. "It truly boggles my mind that you two are related—much less twins." She shook her head and retrieved her coffee, holding it to her chest like Malcolm might come over and steal it.

"Ha! You're delightful. I remember you from last night. I can't seem to recall your name, though. Care to enlighten me?" He made himself at home, pulling up a dining chair and sitting with one leg crossed over his knee.

"Her name is Ruby. Ruby, this is my miscreant brother, Malcolm."

Ruby raised a hand in a lackluster greeting.

"It's lovely to meet you, Ruby. And may I say you have impeccable taste in automobiles. Is she a '65?"

At the mention of Stella, Ruby turned her full attention to Malcolm for the first time since he walked into the apartment. "She is." Her voice held a hint of admiration. "I'm still working on the cosmetic restoration, but the engine is a thing of beauty."

"Indeed. I took the liberty of checking under the hood. I hope you don't mind." Malcolm's smile grew when Ruby shrugged. He dropped his foot to the floor and leaned forward in his chair, elbows resting on his knees. "I've just had the most brilliant idea."

Dread flooded me. Nope. This could not be good. I moved to intercede, but he forged ahead.

"What do you say to a drive down the Blue Ridge Parkway in your beauty of an American classic?" He clapped his hands together. "It couldn't be more perfect!"

Ruby's eyes were mere slits at this point, she'd narrowed them so severely. "I'm sorry. Are you still drunk?"

Malcolm just chuckled. "Hear me out. The weather is perfect, it's only a couple hours from here, and we'd pay you, of course." He still wouldn't look at me.

"Absolutely not," I interjected. "You know we can't do it, Malcolm." I stood, as if this would force him to listen. "And, besides, Ruby has a job—and we're complete strangers!" He waved me off but I continued, "I've already explained all of this to you. It's not time to be inconveniencing a nice person who already did us a favor letting us sleep here last night."

"How much?"

Our eyes shot to Ruby who was now sitting at attention.

What the fuck?

Malcolm's eyes practically sparkled with glee. He didn't even hesitate before answering. "Ten thousand dollars. Half now and half when we return. And we pay for food and lodging."

"Malcolm!" I stepped between the two of them.

"How many days are we talking?" Ruby again.

"We're not—" I began, but Malcolm talked over me.

"Two, maybe three. It depends."

"On what?!" I shouted, the anger burning to my very bones. He couldn't do this!

"Deal." And the final word went to the beautiful girl who had no idea what she was getting herself into.

"Look, I know you didn't manage to get hold of Trevor or I'd have awoken on a plane this morning. And we both know you're never calling Mother. So let's just let this thing play out."

"Absolutely not." I felt as if my neck were developing a sprain from all the shaking it had been doing.

Malcolm grabbed my arm and pulled me farther into the kitchen. "You think I can't read you the same way you can read me? I'm doing you a favor, Leo." He gestured to the next room where Ruby, still in that outfit that made me want to put a blindfold on Mal, spoke on the phone to someone. "You are in serious infatuation mode with this girl and I just scored you several days of intimate proximity. I know you don't like to close the deal on a first date—blah, blah, blah—but even you can score by the end of this little excursion."

I hoped my curled lip accurately expressed my level of revulsion. "You're paying this woman to not only drive us but have sex with me? She's not a chauffeur, Malcolm, and she most definitely is not a prostitute!"

"Calm your nuts. I'm renting her *car*. She's coming along as a safeguard so we don't steal it. If she happens to end up in bed with one of us, all the better."

I growled.

"I'm just taking the piss out of you." He raised a hand. "I promise I'll keep my behavior to mild flirting."

"And what do you plan to do when she realizes we don't have credit cards for hotels? What kind of people travel overseas without credit cards? Or phones?! Do you expect her to just shrug and sleep in the car with us?" I grumbled. "This plan has so many holes."

Malcolm put both hands on my shoulders. "Deep breaths, Leo." I glared at him. "Everything will be fine. Live a little, please."

"Tell that to Trevor and Alice when they get fired." Spending the next few days with Ruby sounded like the best idea on earth—in theory. But, unlike Malcolm, I lived in the real world. I knew he was disappointed in me, but I frankly didn't give a single shit.

The idea that Ruby was clearly in need of money, on the other hand, did concern me. She would never have agreed to this—especially considering her dislike for my brother—if she weren't hard up. I decided then and there to make sure she got the cash, but I was getting Trevor on the bloody phone if it killed me. Malcolm and I were going home, and the lovely Ruby was staying in Kernersville, North Carolina, with some cash in her pocket for being a decent human being.

Mal sighed. "I promise you, nobody is losing their job."

I met his eyes again. "We'll have to agree to disagree on that." I sighed. "Just give me a few minutes to think, okay? I'm going to get Ruby some breakfast that hasn't been on the floor. We can talk more when I get back."

He let go and gave me a final clap on the shoulder.

I walked out the door without a word to Ruby and

hurried down the stairs and out to the street where I couldn't be overheard. I took a deep breath and dialed, letting it out as I punched in the extension and the line picked up.

"What is it now?" the irritated female voice snapped. "And just so you're aware, these calls are recorded."

"Good," I said. "I always do like the sound of my own voice. I hear Leo's been calling and not getting through. Do me a favor, love. Tell Trevor that Malcolm needs to speak to him at this number." I rattled off the ten-digit number I'd memorized. "If he's in any doubt that it's really me, tell him I said the tattoo on his right shoulder makes him look like a complete git and until he stops taking those garlic capsules, he has no hope in hell of getting laid."

She began to stammer but I talked over her.

"And I'll be sure to bring something nice back for you if he gets my message. Cheers." I hung up, breathing like I'd just run a marathon. After a moment, I shoved the phone back in my pocket and crossed the street toward the bakery. Before I even reached the door, the phone rang. I brought it to my ear with a grimace.

Trevor's voice thundered over the line. "Your Highness, pardon my impertinence, but where in the ever-loving FUCK are you?!"

CHAPTER TEN

RUBY

"I'm sure she's fine. She just sounded a bit lonely and I thought she could use a friendly face." I held the phone and lied through my teeth to my uncle. My ticket on the fast train to hell was officially bought and paid for with all the lies I'd been spreading around.

Carl sighed. "I just talked to her a couple days ago and she told me she was doin' great. You don't think this has to do with a guy, do you?" I could practically hear him cracking his knuckles in preparation to teach some college kid a lesson.

"No!" I had to nip that in the bud ASAP. "It's probably just exam stress or something. No biggie. But you'll be okay without me, right?"

"I'll make it work. We can always shuffle appointments

around. Sadie's more important." He grunted. "Thanks for looking out for her. You're a good kid, Ruby."

Ugh. I mimed stabbing myself in the chest and bleeding out, and then peeked behind me to make sure neither of the Baxter brothers had seen me. But they were in the kitchen having their own conversation.

To say I was bowled over by Malcolm's gazillion dollar offer was like saying a '69 Boss 429 Mustang would be an *okay* ride. And, yeah, maybe it wasn't exactly a gazillion dollars, but to me, it may as well have been. Who has ten thousand dollars to throw around like candy?

There was definitely more to these guys than the homeless and hapless impression I'd gotten thus far. It was also clear they didn't agree on the details of this trip, but I was siding with Malcolm if it got me the money—regardless of the fact he'd been such an asshole the night before. I had pride, but I apparently also had a price, and ten thousand was it. And, sure, I was curious as hell, but nothing was more important than getting that money, so I was keeping my trap shut till that cash was in my pocket. If that meant a road trip with the charming Hottie Van Moneybags and his drunken pervy brother, then sign me the hell up!

I said my goodbyes to Carl, silently apologizing for lying to him and then hopped my way to my bedroom to put some real clothes on. My boobs had made enough of an appearance for one day. A pair of cutoffs and a black cherry bomb t-shirt did the trick. My next stop was the bathroom to finally brush my teeth and take some more ibuprofen. I may have also fixed my hair and put on a touch of makeup, but that's my prerogative, so I don't want to hear it.

When I hobbled back out to the living room, Malcolm

was seated on my couch paging through a copy of *Hemming's Muscle Machines* he must have found lying around. I looked to the kitchen, but there was no sign of Leo. My heart picked up a panicked beat as it occurred to me he may have found his friend and left. He had said they were waiting for their ride. Disappointment and hurt ran through me at having missed the chance to see him one last time and say goodbye.

"Where's your brother?" I had to ask.

"He's playing the gentleman and buying you some fresh baked goods. I made a judgment call and tossed the other ones. I hope you don't mind."

Relief washed through me. I shook my head in response to Malcolm but his eyes were riveted on the magazine. I pressed my teeth into my lower lip. Leo was getting me another bear claw. He hadn't left. I considered the notion that I might be in some serious trouble. This guy was polite, sweet, rich, *and* hot. Granted, he could also be a mob boss for all I knew, but consider the seeds of this crush planted, watered, and sprinkled with a generous helping of Miracle-Gro. And I'd be spending the next few days riding next to him with Stella's top down and the mountains creating the perfect backdrop. I was living in a freaking Marilyn Monroe movie. And getting paid to be there!

My attention came back to Malcolm. Right. I doubted Marilyn had anyone quite like him as a co-star. Oh well. It was probably for the best, I had to remind myself.

"I have this one, you know. Back at home." Malcolm's eyes finally rose from the page and I came closer to see what he was pointing at. His index finger rested next to an image of a 1965 Shelby GT350R.

"No, you don't." It wasn't a question.

One side of his mouth turned up. "Yes, I do." He sat forward and reached for the back of his jeans. "Damn."

"What?"

"My phone. I was going to show you a picture, but I don't have my phone."

I set aside the Shelby for a moment, though I promised myself we'd get right back to that. I mean, there was no way he was being straight with me. "Okay, I have to ask. No phone? No car? Seriously?" I couldn't help it. I didn't want to pry and risk my paycheck, but these were some huge freaking red flags. Maybe this was some big joke and there was no money.

He squinted and set the magazine aside. "Let's just say we're roughing it." He pointed to his clothes as proof.

Okay, that was fair. I tried to ignore his shirt, hoping to God he would change before I had to be seen in public with him. "But you have buckets of money to hand out to girls for a ride in their cars?"

He thought about it for a moment before answering with a simple, "Yes."

I sat my butt on the arm of the couch. I doubted any more answers would be forthcoming. "Fine by me. So, any idea when I might be getting that cash? Not to be pushy or anything." I added a bright smile so I didn't come off as a greedy bitch.

His eyes brightened. "Absolutely!" Then his hand disappeared into first his right pocket and then his left. The lightness on his face died as he groaned and his head dropped into his hands. "Fuck!"

My head fell back. I *knew* it was too good to be true.

Why did I never learn that guys with smiles like the Baxter brothers' were not to be trusted? The only things they brought were disappointment and a bucketful of regret. I could only blame myself, though. I'd gotten my hopes up over something ridiculous.

Well, forget it. I was sending these boys on their way back to whatever international halfway house they'd crawled out of and I was going back to Benny's tonight to make some connections. I'd forgotten the lesson I'd been taught time and again—most guys are bastards. I rose without a word and hopped over to grab my purse. I pulled out a twenty and made my way back to the couch where Malcolm still had his face buried in his hands and was making moaning sounds.

"Here." I held out the bill, but he didn't look up. "Here!" That got his attention, and I almost tripped backward over the coffee table at the look in his eyes when they drifted upward. Gone was the cocky smartass with impulse-control issues. He was now the picture of dejection and utter defeat.

He blinked a few times and his eyes finally settled on the twenty. "What is this?"

I forced an eye-roll. "Money. You obviously don't have any. Maybe this will get you a hot meal or bus fare. I don't know. Just take it." I shook it for emphasis.

His blue gaze flicked back and forth from the bill to my face. "You're giving me twenty dollars?"

I huffed, pulling the money back and crossing my arms. "It's not like I have that much to spare. A simple thank you would have done."

He shook his head sharply. "No. I didn't mean it that

way. It's just ... that's a really nice thing to do." He stood then and ran a hand through his hair. His eyes swept my apartment and I couldn't read the new expression he wore. When his gaze met mine again, he offered a sad little smile. "You're a nice girl, Ruby. Truly."

I opened my mouth to respond, not sure what I was going to say, but Leo strolled through the apartment door before I had to figure it out. Unfortunately, he looked just as tempting as he had before I found out he was shady, and in his hand was another white bakery bag. I just hoped he hadn't stolen the bear claw for me. His smile fell when he saw Malcolm and me standing across from one another, a stillness in the air.

"What's wrong?"

Malcolm winced and stepped to the other side of the coffee table in an apparent attempt to create distance between Leo and himself. Leo dropped the bag on the kitchen table and set his hands on his hips. "What now?" I gathered this exchange wasn't a new one between these two.

Malcolm held his hands out in defense. "Before you go all Hulk on me, I'll start by saying I'm sorry."

Leo stepped closer, needing no words to get his message across as Malcolm took another step back.

"I lost the money." Malcolm cringed at his own words. But one look at Leo showed only raised eyebrows.

What the hell was going on?! Was the money real?

Then Leo reached into the front pocket of his dirty jeans and pulled out a large folded stack of bills. I stared.

"Asshole!!" Malcolm shouted and took a running jump, using the coffee table to launch himself over the couch and right into his brother. They both fell to the floor in a tangle of elbows, fists, neon pink, and curses. The cash went flying and I found myself standing in a virtual pasture of money the likes of which I'd never seen.

I lowered myself to the floor with my feet splayed out and began tidying it up, dazed by the numbers I was counting. The brothers continued their scuffle and I let them be while I finished. Then I pulled myself up, crossed to the kitchen table and set down two stacks of bills, one on either side of the bakery bag. I reached in, grabbed my bear claw and took a huge sticky bite, not caring when the glaze fell on my t-shirt and floor. I chewed the sugary treat, swallowed and smacked my lips before using my fingers to belt out a deafening whistle, just like Carl had taught me.

Both brothers stilled, their eyes coming up to me. Bear claw in one hand and a stack of cash equaling five freaking thousand dollars in the other, I smiled.

"Let's hit the road, boys."

By the time the guys got over their argument and stopped with the insults, I had two missed calls from Sadie and a couple added threatening text messages. I knew I had to call her, if for no other reason than to get her to cover for me with Uncle Carl, but I honestly didn't know what to tell her without spilling the details about Jason. So I waited while doing my best to formulate a plan.

Malcolm, in his sly manner, somehow convinced me to hand over Stella's keys so he could run to the shopping center and grab some new clothes for them and an ankle brace for me. Leo was to act as collateral. Well, Leo and the money Malcolm hadn't taken with him. Truthfully, it was the thought of their grimy jeans sullying Stella's upholstery for the rest of the day that made the decision for me. She didn't deserve that.

So while Malcolm shopped, I packed a small bag and let Leo use my shower. My apartment was not huge, and the wall shared by the bathroom and my bedroom wasn't the most soundproof thing in the world. Which meant that while I sifted through my underwear drawer deciding on what to pack, the sounds of water splashing over Leo's naked body all but assaulted me. I felt a line of sweat form above my upper lip. I considered turning the air conditioning on but determined that would be silly since we'd be leaving in just a bit.

When I heard what sounded distinctly like a groan I slammed the drawer shut, my eyes going to the ceiling in a silent plea for help of some kind. My mind conjured various scenarios, none of them working to cool me down in the least. What was wrong with me? I was acting like a dog in heat just because a hot guy was washing himself. In my shower. With my soap. Good Christ, I was a mess. I opened another drawer and shoved random clothes from it into my canvas bag.

Leo wasn't a particularly large guy. He was probably five-foot-ten or eleven and not overly bulky, but more of a leanly-muscled sort. It was clear he worked out in some form because every time he moved his arms in that white t-shirt, his biceps had popped out. And I'd be lying if I said I didn't get a peek at his abdomen when he and Malcolm had been tussling on my kitchen floor. There was some definition there for sure, along with the perfect sprinkling of dark hair leading into his low-slung jeans. And that didn't even take into account the ass I'd checked out earlier.

Yes, it was safe to say my shower was hosting quite the sexy male specimen just a handful of yards from where my bag and I stood. I took a breath and let it out slowly. Down, girl.

I made quick work with the rest of my packing, only allowing the briefest sigh when I bypassed my heels in favor of Converse. But I was a practical woman and this ankle needed a few days' rest from anything that cute. I also managed to keep my thoughts from any splashing or sluicing or dripping sounds coming through the wall— mostly. But, honestly, what was he doing in there that made so much noise?

Finally, the water shut off, just as I zipped my bag and hobbled to the hallway.

That was when the bathroom door opened, and sweet lord in heaven, Leo Baxter stood in the doorway with his lower half wrapped in a towel and beads of water clinging to the ends of his thick hair and eyelashes. My ovaries folded their hands under their chins and sighed.

"That was, hands down, the best shower I've ever had." Leo stretched his neck from side to side, seemingly unbothered by his state of undress.

"Me too." Those were the words that came out of my mouth.

His head straightened and he got that little V between his brows.

I felt myself blush—and I *never* blush. "I mean, I have great water pressure," I quickly amended.

The corner of his mouth quirked. "That you do." And then his eyes swept down my form, heating more than just my face. Was he seriously making innuendo about my water fixtures? And if so, why was it working for me?

Taking advantage of the moment, I returned the favor of the body sweep, shamelessly letting my eyes linger on his bare chest and stomach. This boy was sex on a stick, and he didn't even seem to know it.

I felt his hand touch my hair, taking a lock gently between his fingers. My eyes closed and his hand moved to my face, taking my cheek in his palm. Everything south of my lungs clenched. He must have stepped closer because I could feel his soft breath on my face. The sound of my bag hitting the floor was the only thing telling me I'd dropped it. Every cell was attuned to this man, his closeness, his scent. The barest touch of his lips on mine had me leaning in and capturing that full lower lip between my own. God, his skin was warm, his lips smooth and soft. A drop of water ran down my temple from his hair, and one of his hands slid to the back of my neck, the dual sensation sending lightning down my spine.

The opening notes of "Fastest Girl in Town" blared from the bag at our feet and we jumped apart like two teenagers caught parking. Our breaths came out in pants as we looked down at my bag. I also couldn't help but notice the tent formed by the towel and whatever Leo was packing under there. I didn't reach for the phone, only partly because bending over would put me face-to-crotch with Leo, and his brother could be back any second. That might prove a tad awkward. Also, I did *not* want to talk to

Sadie right then. What I really wanted was to go back to the kissing thing.

Recognizing one aspect of my predicament, Leo practically leapt back, putting space between us and breaking what was left of the mood. His next words put the nails in its coffin. "Is Malcolm back?"

It took me a moment, but I shook my head, both to clear it and to answer his question. The song on my phone stopped as Sadie's call went to voicemail.

Leo's feet shifted on the tiles and he ran a hand through his wet hair, causing droplets of water to scatter and drawing my eyes to his bicep again. I hadn't even gotten to touch it yet. Damn. "Listen, Ruby." He paused, and my gaze met his as I refocused my mind. "I need to tell you something."

No good story ever started with that line. I was the one to take a step back this time, and Leo noticed.

"It's not about the money," he was quick to reassure. "I promise we're not bullshitting you on that. You can have the full ten thousand right now as far as I'm concerned." His hand was back in his hair.

I wanted to feel relieved, but I didn't. "Then what is it?" A knot formed in my stomach. "You're not involving me in something illegal, are you?"

"No!" He shook his head so hard it had more water flying about. "It's about the trip."

My phone chose that moment to, yet again, belt out "Fastest Girl in Town." I couldn't decide who to yell at first —Sadie or Miranda Lambert.

I didn't take my eyes off Leo. But he seemed to have lost track, or maybe nerve. "Aren't you going to get that?"

"It's just my cousin. I'll call her later."

Leo shifted once more, and it was clear he wasn't ready to share until I answered the damn phone. And Sadie wasn't about to stop calling either, so I unzipped my bag and brought the cursed device to my ear.

"Can I call you later?"

"Ruby! No, you can't call me later! You have some hot foreign guy knocking on your door and then you don't return my calls for two hours ..." The wind left her sails as she changed tones. "Ooooooh." I could see the misguided lightbulb switching on in her brain. "Oh my God. I'm so sorry! Carry on with whatever you're doing and call me later with all the details!"

If only. But that ship had sailed, at least for the moment. I fought the urge to laugh. "Sadie! Jesus. It's not that." I was becoming a pro at this fibbing thing.

"Oh. Bummer."

I smiled. "I'm just working on something." There, that wasn't a lie.

The apartment door opened, turning my head as Malcolm's voice came bellowing into the space. "I come bearing new clothes, an ankle wrap, crutches, a large bottle of Jack Daniels, and something called Cheerwine. Blue Ridge Parkway, here we come!"

I hung my head.

"Girl! Don't you even *think* about hanging up on me!"

I was finally granted permission to hang up once plans had been made to stop and see Sadie on our way. As she'd pointed out, we'd be driving right near Boone and App State anyway, and this way I wouldn't be lying as badly to her dad.

I'd somehow managed to make the trip sound like I just had an overwhelming urge to do something impulsive and a road trip with two hot brothers fit the bill. There was no mention of the money or Jason, thank God.

Leo was strangely quiet and fidgety while Malcolm showered, and any attempt to engage him in conversation failed. I eventually gave up and just peeked his way every couple minutes to check him out. He was dressed in new jeans and a navy-blue Captain America t-shirt, his dark hair now dry but in disarray. A few locks curled in front of his ear and one had fallen over his forehead, making me want to go over and brush it back. His attention seemed fixed on the street outside my window. Was he going to bail on the trip after all? I wanted to know what he'd been about to say outside the bathroom, but I was almost afraid to ask. I mean, for the money, I'd still go with Malcolm, but I'd feel safer with Leo—and a whole lot happier. And hornier.

The sounds of "Country Roads" sung in an off-key voice came from the bathroom, making me laugh and finally drawing Leo's attention from the window.

I was packing some snacks in Malcolm's paper grocery bag in the kitchen, my ankle newly wrapped and my shoes on, making my steps feel vastly more supported. "I'm actually getting excited about this trip," I shared, unsure if Leo would even hear me. "The mountains really are beautiful, and the weather is perfect."

More lyrics spilled from the bathroom, this time with the tune the same, but the words made up—something about driving with my brother and a girl from Carolina and definitely not West Virginia. He continued with another line about last chances and making memories.

"Goddammit!" Leo strode to the bathroom door, mouth tight. Apparently, the song wasn't as amusing to Leo as it was to me. Something was really eating at him. I craned my neck to see him pound on the door.

"Mal!"

The singing stopped. "What?!"

Leo turned to me then, his jaw set. "How fast can we be out the door?"

My brow furrowed, and I looked down first at my packed bag and then the snacks. I shrugged. "I'm ready when you are."

He spared me a ghost of a smile and thumped his forehead on the bathroom door. The shower turned off.

"What?" came Malcolm's voice again.

Leo's head lifted off the door and I could see his chest expand with his inhale. "If you don't want to be on a plane back home today, you'd best get your arse moving. Trevor is on his way and I don't think we have much time."

I had no earthly idea what any of that meant, but by the cursing coming from inside my bathroom, I guessed it wasn't good. Nope, not good at all.

CHAPTER ELEVEN

LEO

I wasn't unaware that my behavior was like a yo-yo. I'd been steadfastly determined not an hour before, but the combination of that kiss, the looks Ruby had been shooting at me, and Malcolm's damn singing in the shower had undone me. If I knew Trevor, he'd be breaking every speed limit in the country to get here as fast as humanly possible, Alice waving traffic off in the passenger seat the whole way. The guilt still ate at me, but it came from two directions, and I'd finally made my choice. I'd make things right somehow with Trevor, Alice, and anyone else we'd wronged, but I had a gut feeling things between Malcolm and me would never be quite the same if I didn't do this.

Ruby covered her eyes as Mal tore around the apartment in his new boxers, grabbing things as he went and trying to pull the rest of his clothes on. I quickly scribbled a note for Trevor and helped Ruby down the stairs before running back up and grabbing the rest of her things. Then I memorized Trevor's number from the call earlier and set both the note and the burner phone by the front door to the shop.

I tried sending reassuring smiles to Ruby as she sat perched in the Mustang's passenger seat looking both stunningly beautiful and worried. I didn't blame her. I was a nervous wreck.

I'd been trying not to let my thoughts travel back to our encounter outside her bathroom, as I'd been anticipating parting ways and didn't have room in my mind for more regret. But knowing I'd have a few more days with her now, I was unable to keep my head from going places—tempting places.

The look on her face, surprised and unguarded, when I'd opened the bathroom door had crumbled every bit of my restraint. I could read her so clearly, and it was gratifying to know this attraction I felt didn't go just one way. Her eyes were hungry and I knew mine reflected the same look. Nothing could have stopped me from leaning in for that kiss. And the feel of her lips on mine was nothing short of perfect. Until her phone rang and I got my wits about me.

It wasn't as if women had never been attracted to me before. I wasn't oblivious. And I had engaged in both brief affairs and relationships over the years. But I'd never felt quite the same physical pull toward another woman. If I hadn't been embroiled in this out-of-control escapade with Malcolm, I would have already done my best to get Ruby to spend a week locked in her apartment together. Well, that probably wasn't true. The deception didn't sit well with me, and I'd hate to imagine how I might hurt her with it.

Ironically, the fact that she hadn't a clue as to my title helped me trust my impression of her. My younger self had been burned more than a few times by women who cared more for the prestige of being on my arm than being with me. It had been a hard lesson to learn, but over the years I'd gotten quite skilled at spotting royal groupies and it was a relief to not have that to consider. Not that anything would happen between us anyway, with only a day or two ahead of us. Still, it was nice to have a place to let my mind wander when I had the urge to let my fantasies run wild.

Despite Malcolm's plans for Ruby and me, I was determined to keep things from going too far. Two days was not long enough for the things I'd like to do, and there was absolutely no possibility of a relationship of any kind. I was going home and she was staying here. I shook my head at myself. I'd known the woman for less than a day and I was already experiencing regret at the impossibility of a future.

Footsteps pounded down the stairs and I started the engine. Malcolm threw a bag in the backseat and Ruby handed over the garage keys, instructing him to secure the place while I backed out of the bay. My heart thundered in my chest and I could see Ruby worrying her lip beside me, her long leg jittering on the seat. Her stress level must have been about as high as mine because she didn't even scold Malcolm when he hoisted himself over the side of the car and into the backseat, his shoe landing on the upholstery.

"Go!" He shouted, and I shifted the car in gear and tore out of the lot, barely managing to keep the tires from squealing. We held our communal breath for the first minute or two until we were safely away from the garage and heading toward the highway.

Ruby directed me to US-421, and the moment I merged from the on-ramp and into the flow of cars, Malcolm let out a wild whooping cry and Ruby threw her head back and laughed, the sound hitting me in the chest in the best of ways. I felt my face break into a broad smile as I glanced back and forth between Ruby, Malcolm, and the road ahead.

It felt like we were in a classic film, rolling down the highway in a bright red convertible, a gorgeous girl in the passenger seat. I had the urge to thank Malcolm for his impulsive nature and disregard for rules, but I wasn't about to go that far.

With the road noise and the wind whipping around us, conversation was pointless, and it wasn't long before Ruby snapped on the radio and American country music wailed from the speakers. I'd heard it before, of course, but knowing Ruby favored it automatically opened my mind to it. Three songs in, and I was itching to ask if all country songs featured beer and pickup trucks or if we'd just stumbled upon these themes by coincidence. The fourth song dispelled that thought, but also introduced a new theme of drunk-dialing into the mix. It continued in this manner as we made our way west through Winston-Salem where Malcolm insisted we stop.

"Cigarettes!" he declared, gesturing for me to pull off at the exit.

Unsure if he'd suddenly developed Tourette's Syndrome, I did as he asked, noting the petrol could use topping off anyway.

"Since when do you smoke?" I turned in the seat as we waited at a red light.

"You're not smoking in this car, just so you know." Ruby sifted through her black polka-dotted purse and didn't bother looking at my brother. "I know I'm not done restoring the interior, but I'm holding firm on that."

"I wouldn't dream of it, Ruby," Malcolm reassured. "And I don't smoke."

That turned Ruby's head, her hand stilling in her purse. "Then why the hell did you scream 'Cigarettes!'?" She perfectly mocked his tone and shook her head at him. "You're getting stranger by the minute, I swear."

This made me smile as I took in her adorable scowl and her wind-blown hair that had escaped her hair tie.

"We're in Winston-Salem. I consider it my duty to purchase cigarettes when an entire city shares the brand name. Two brand names!" His eyes moved to me. "It would be like visiting Dunwall without purchasing a Dunwall pie."

He did have a point. I turned back and drove forward as the light switched to green.

"You have pie named after your hometown?" Ruby resumed the search through her purse, finally extracting a red kerchief and folding it in her lap.

"Not just any pie. The best pie," I told her.

She shot me a look, and I could have sworn it carried a hint of intimacy—or maybe I was reading into things because I wanted to. "Hmm. I guess every town is known for something. What flavor is this famous Dunwall pie?"

"Lamb," Malcolm and I spoke at once.

Ruby's lip curled. "Oh. *That* kind of pie."

Malcolm scoffed and I shot her a look. "What do you mean, '*That* kind of pie'? Have you ever had lamb pie?"

"I can safely say the answer is no. I thought you were talking about a fruit pie or a cream pie or something. You know, a dessert." She continued to fold the cloth into a band.

"I'm beginning to comprehend the extreme nature of your sweet tooth."

She grinned, folding the kerchief one last time and bringing it around to the back of her neck. "It's a real issue."

I pulled into a petrol station and Malcolm hopped out even before I'd come to a full stop. He apparently was in desperate need of those cigarettes.

"Besides, I don't eat lamb." Ruby adjusted the side mirror and used it to help her tie her hair back with the red cloth. I watched her movements, mesmerized by the simple actions and feeling the urge to stroke her hair like a creeper.

"Oh, is that not an American thing?" I forced a casual air.

"It is, I suppose." She tucked a last lock of hair back before returning the mirror to its original position and looking my way. "Just not for me. I don't like to eat any animal that's not full grown. I don't eat veal either." She shrugged. "It kind of makes me think of eating a puppy." Her nose scrunched, bringing my attention to her freckles.

I choked. "But you'd eat a full-grown Labrador, say?"

She laughed, the sound going to my gut. "Probably not."

I opened the door to get out but couldn't help throwing one last glance her way, taking in her smile. Damn, she was pretty. "Be right back."

I hurried into the station and paid cash for the petrol. Malcolm was deep in conversation with one of the attendants about American cigarettes and I'm not sure that he even noticed me. When I returned to the car and began pumping the gas, I took a few steps to the side and held my breath.

Noticing my behavior, Ruby shot me a puzzled look. "Why are you holding your breath?"

"Petrol fumes," I croaked.

She looked toward the boot where the fuel dispenser protruded from the car. "It can't be that bad." She laughed at the look on my face. I suppose it would seem ridiculous to a woman who works on cars for a living. "I'm sure you have gas pumps at home." Her eyebrows shot up. "Or do you have *people* who pump your gas for you, Mister Pocket-O-Cash?"

We did, in fact, have such people, but I wasn't about to admit that to her. It wasn't the point, anyway.

"He drives an electric car," Malcolm inserted himself into the conversation, striding our way.

"Seriously?"

I let out my breath and barely kept from coughing. "As a matter of fact, I do." I shot a glare at Malcolm. "It's the globally responsible thing to do."

Ruby looked at Malcolm and, after a beat, they both burst out laughing.

I didn't know why I even tried.

We threaded our way through the winding roads of Boone,

North Carolina. We'd finally reached Mal's beloved (*cough*) Blue Ridge Mountains. The air was cooler in the mountains, but it felt more refreshing than anything. We were on our way to meet Ruby's cousin for a late lunch. She attended the local university called Appalachian State, the mention of which prompted protests from Malcolm based on his only experience with the word Appalachian.

Following Ruby's lecture about not relying on Holly-wood movies for accurate reflections on regional culture, he finally agreed to come along. He did, however, threaten to ditch us if the sound of a banjo reached his ears at any point. I was tempted to tell him that his damn Blue Ridge Mountains were actually part of the Appalachian Mountains but figured that would be pushing too much. He finally settled back, muttering about his lingering hopes to find some good local moonshine. It was a wonder Ruby didn't dump him on the highway.

"So, you mean you make those giant white windmills I see on the internet all the time?"

It had only been a matter of time before Ruby started wanting to know more personal details about us, and I had to admit, it felt good to be on the receiving end of any interest from her. She'd already quizzed us about our country of origin, and I was relieved when the Feldlands only warranted a passing, "Oh."

"No, I don't actually manufacture them, but my degree is in civil engineering and I'm working on the government project commissioning them." I didn't mention the project was *mine*, or that our country's green initiative was my one true passion.

"My brother is intent on making the earth last long

enough for hundreds of generations. I, on the other hand, am a bit more focused on the now, as you might have guessed."

"Wow." Ruby looked impressed, which I admit made my chest swell a bit. "So, it's safe to say you don't have a Hummer in your driveway back home."

I sent her a dark look, but it seemed to amuse her.

"He's no saint, Ruby dear. Don't let him fool you. He's been known to take a ride in my Aston Martin once in a while."

Ruby's jaw dropped and all her attention transferred to Malcolm. A bolt of jealousy cut through me before I could stop it. "Wait. You have a Shelby *and* an Aston Martin?"

I was tempted to choose this moment to tell Malcolm that he may no longer own that Aston Martin when we returned home, but I refrained. Barely.

"I do, indeed. As well as a few more toys you may have heard of." As Malcolm rattled off his list of cars and Ruby grew more incredulous at each name, I wracked my brain for something that might interest her more than his collection. However, it was difficult to make solar panels and windmills sound sexy, no matter how I might try.

My mood having turned, I hardly paid attention to their conversation as the GPS from Ruby's phone directed me to the restaurant and the car came to a stop in the lot across the street. I'd been so inattentive that I hadn't realized they'd both stopped talking and were looking at me.

"What?" I had an urge to check if I had bird shit on my head.

"You really did that?" Ruby asked.

"Did what?" I hadn't a clue what they were on about.

"Daydreaming, brother?" I caught Malcolm's wink in the rearview mirror. "I was just telling Ruby about the charity auctions you organize to dig wells for all those villages in Bangladesh or wherever it is."

Oh.

I felt my face begin to heat at her focused attention.

"Well, it certainly isn't a one-man job." I almost stumbled over the words, my hands gripping the steering wheel to give them an occupation.

"But still, that's amazing." Her smile was dazzling.

I wanted to groan. If she only knew how easy these things were to do when you had money and influence, she wouldn't be so impressed. That was the problem. There is always more we can do. This knowledge rules my life, for the most part. It was the main reason I'd wanted to go home so badly and hadn't even wished to come on the trip in the first place.

"Did you go to Bangladesh? To see the wells?"

I nodded. I had gone, mostly to ensure everything went as planned and the teams followed the instruction of the hydrogeologist I'd hired. Too many of these wells were drying up the underground aquifers and I didn't want that happening to our adopted villages if it could be avoided. "It was amazing." It truly had been, in so many ways. Trips like that reminded me why I was lucky to be born to a royal family, and why I had a responsibility to the rest of the world.

But I couldn't tell her any of that, although I had the strongest urge to just come clean and let it all spill out. Would she still smile at me like that?

"Ruby!" an excited feminine voice pealed from the

sidewalk and a lovely girl with long blond hair and a flowing skirt nearly skipped to the Mustang. She halted a few yards away, her eyes moving back and forth between Malcolm and me. "I knew—I mean, in my head, it was one thing—but in person it's a whole other thing!" Her hands circled the air.

I wasn't sure what in the bloody hell she was talking about, but Ruby sure found it amusing. She dropped her chin and chuckled before holding her arms out. "Come here and give me a hug, woman!"

The girl's attention went back to her cousin and she squealed as she closed the distance and fell on Ruby, arms wrapping and squeezing around her cousin in unfiltered enthusiasm. She whispered something unintelligible which triggered another round of giggles. I turned in my seat to see Malcolm's attention riveted on the two females, dirty fantasies no doubt playing out in his mind. I shook my head and opened the door.

The restaurant had a casual, if not flannel, vibe with dark wood booths lining the walls and a main bar curving around the center portion of the space. Chatter from the diners peppered the air, and music mixed in to create a lively atmosphere.

Introductions had been made once Ruby extracted herself from Sadie's embrace and tolerated her cousin's fawning over her injury. I carefully assisted Ruby across the uneven gravel of the lot with her new crutches, and if I'd thought Ruby's expressions transparent, they were nothing compared to Sadie's. The girl practically glowed as she took in every one of my actions toward her cousin. But I couldn't help myself, and if my instincts garnered awkward attention, so be it. Ruby did elbow me good-naturedly when I made a move to lift her bodily up the curb in front of the restaurant. My innocent look was met with an eye-roll and another giggle from Sadie.

We were seated at a booth, and no sooner had we ordered our drinks when Sadie dragged Ruby off to the loo in a manner almost as subtle as Malcolm's t-shirt from the previous night.

"The cousin's quite the hot one, isn't she? You know I'm fond of all the youthful exuberance."

"Don't even think about it." I unrolled my cutlery from the paper napkin and determined to ignore his remark.

"What? So you get Ruby and I don't even get to enjoy a nice breath of fresh air?" He leaned back on his side of the booth, adopting his signature casual posture.

"First of all, I'm not *getting* Ruby. We'll be parting ways in a matter of hours really, so what is the point?" I pressed a crease into the napkin, feeling disproportionately frustrated.

Malcolm seemed almost personally offended. "I orchestrated this entire trip so you could score with the lovely Ruby and you're not even going to give it your best shot?"

That bought him a glare. "Mal, please don't pretend this trip is about anyone but you."

He shrugged but didn't comment.

I got back to my point. "And second, I'd guess Sadie's age to be maybe twenty-one. Do not go there. Besides, I get the sense Ruby would likely produce a tire iron and beat you savagely if you so much as glanced in her cousin's direction." I formed another crease with my restless fingers. At this rate, I'd have an origami bird by the time the women returned.

He considered that. "You do have a point. Oh well, at least I have memories of the dueling vaginas to take home with me." The waitress chose that moment to bring our drinks, saving me from reaching over the table to smack the back of my brother's head.

"What do you think they're talking about in there?" Malcolm shot a glance to the back of the restaurant where the girls had disappeared.

"If I had to guess, I'd say Ruby is warning Sadie off of you." I enjoyed the look on Malcolm's face at that.

"No. I think they're deciding which of us is the finer specimen. Please accept my condolences in advance." He bowed his head and I tossed the mangled napkin at his face.

"Or they could be simply using the loo."

"God, you're a buzz kill." Malcolm lifted his water glass to his mouth and took a deep swallow.

"Well, then, I may as well go for broke. I need to know the timeline of this trip so I can buy another phone and check in with Trevor." I held up a hand when Malcolm began to protest. "Not to tell him where we are, just when and where to meet up again. It's the least we can do."

He assumed a bored expression and set his glass back down. "It'll take as long as it takes."

"I can't even imagine an answer less helpful." I sighed. "Look, if we go north on the Parkway, we can stay overnight somewhere—in the correct mountain range this time—get a nice day's drive in and have him meet us somewhere in

Virginia. We can pay someone to drive Ruby home and we'll catch a plane home before we're disinherited. I think that's the best plan."

Malcolm studied me for a long moment, taking in my face and my restless fingers as they tapped the table top, no longer having the napkin to play with. When he finally spoke, it was less than satisfying. "Let me think it over and we'll see."

I don't know why I expected a concrete answer, but there was no time to argue. The girls were back. Sadie's attempt at casual was overreaching at best, and Ruby wore a completely indiscernible expression. One thing was clear, though. Any trace of Ruby's easy manner and openness was long gone. I groaned inwardly.

I was making a new rule—from now on, only one woman was allowed in the loo at a time.

CHAPTER TWELVE

RUBY

After the fact, I felt pretty damn stupid, but my first instinct after meeting someone isn't typically to internet stalk them as soon as their back is turned. I'm more of a form-my-own-opinion kind of girl. And, besides, most of the people I meet wouldn't come up on a Google search unless it was one for criminal records or maybe a hot-dog-eating contest. Sadie, on the other hand? She'd probably give Google a blow job if it were a guy.

Our awkward departure from the table had been typical Sadie, but I was happy to see her so I didn't even give her a hard time. But when she'd turned around after dragging me and my gimpy ankle into the bathroom, I thought the girl might actually pee her pants.

"Oh, Jesus God on a unicycle! Do you know who those guys are?"

I was tempted to lead her into a stall and pull her damn underwear down for her. "Uh, yeah. And so do you. I just introduced you. Are you high?" I leaned into my crutches and almost laughed but she looked like she was on the verge of a panic attack. She inhaled slowly and I was happy she did because I didn't have a paper bag handy.

"Let me rephrase. Do you know anything about Malcolm and Leo Baxter apart from their names and their hometown?"

I smiled, despite myself, and looked down at my Converse. "Well, yeah. A little. Leo builds wells for villages in Bangladesh and he's working on a huge green energy program in the Feldlands. He's also really smart and nice and has kind of a perfect body and entirely perfect hair and I'm having a bit of a hard time not kissing him every time he gets within three feet of me." I didn't look up before continuing. "Oh, and Malcolm's a bit of a pervy asshole, but he grows on you." I shrugged at that because it was just the truth.

Sadie didn't respond so I finally lifted my head and met her eyes. I immediately regretted sharing.

She had big brown puppy eyes. "Oh my God! You totally like this Leo guy."

I did. She was right. But it didn't matter. My smile died on my face and I shook my head. "It doesn't matter, Sadie. He's going home in a couple days and I'm going back to Kernersville and life will go on as usual." I neglected to add the part about me selling either drugs or Stella.

"He's a prince," she said, apropos of nothing at all.

I shot her a dubious look. "I don't know that I'd go that far, but he's definitely a great guy." I couldn't help my inner swoon. Some cool chick I was—my knees were practically buckling at the simple memory of an almost-kiss.

"They're both princes."

I choked out a laugh and crutched my way to the opposite wall. "Okay, you *are* high if you think Malcolm is a prince. I'm sure he's got some swampland and a couple bridges to sell you if you're that easy to fool."

Sadie approached, thumbs to her phone. She turned the screen around to face me. There, in living freaking color, was a picture of Leo and Malcolm dressed in sharp-ass suits standing beside a distinguished-looking older couple and a girl in an elegant gown. Above the photo was the headline, "Prince Malcolm to Take the Throne in the Wake of King Gregory's Declining Health."

My eyes went wide, reading the headline again and then darting around the small room in panic. What the hell?! They found Sadie once more and hers were just as big, except with excitement and not terror like mine. "This is a joke, right?"

One firm shake. "I swear to you, it is not a joke. When we hung up this morning, I got curious. You know me. As soon as I entered Leo's full name, BOOM!" Her free hand smacked the phone.

"This is impossible." I began to crutch and pace. "How have I never heard of these guys? Two hot twin princes? I mean, come on. There would have already been at least ten reality TV shows based on them. Gossip rags, sexiest-princes-alive blue ribbons! Shrines! Something!"

Sadie shrugged and tucked her phone back in her satchel as I crutched my way by her. "Okay, answer me this. Who is the Prince of Liechtenstein?" Her eyes followed me.

I scrubbed a hand over my face, dropping a crutch in the process and not caring one bit. "I don't know! I didn't even know they had a prince or a queen or whatever."

She held up a finger. "Exactly. It's a tiny country, low profile and not a big player on the world stage." She ticked the attributes off as she lifted another finger for each one. "The answer is Prince Hans-Adam II, by the way. I looked it up after finding your hitchhikers." She bent and picked up the crutch.

"Shit. Shit. Shit." I threw my hand out. "What am I supposed to do now?"

Sadie put the crutch under her arm and began hopping her way around the restroom, having a grand old time while I slowly developed an aneurysm. "I don't know. At least you know they're not serial killers now."

I narrowed my eyes at her. "Haha. What have I gotten myself into? And what were they doing in K-ville anyway? I swear, I am the queen of wrong place, wrong time."

"Ha! Queen!"

She got a death glare. "So, what? I'm just supposed to go out there and be like, 'Hey, hop in the backseat of my car, Your Majesty. Oh, and by the way, sorry about the mildew in my shower this morning. If I'd known you were stopping by I'd have called the maid.'?"

Both hands shot up to cover my face and I heard the second crutch hit the tile floor with a clang. "Oh my God! I saw them both practically naked!"

I heard her hopping cease. "Say what?! You've been holding out on me, girl!"

I peeled my hands back and leaned against the wall before I fell. "Can I get in trouble for that? Are they going to make me sign something?" Ten more thoughts rushed through my brain at once. "Stella doesn't even have airbags! What if we got into an accident and I killed a world leader?!" I was the one in need of a paper bag now.

"Calm down." Sadie retrieved the other crutch and handed them both over. I was a freaking mess. "Nothing bad is going to happen." She petted my hair like I was a dog. And, dammit, it helped, so I let her continue. "I've been thinking about this. There has to be a good reason they haven't told you, and I'm guessing it's a pretty simple one."

I stared pleadingly at her, needing a dose of simple right about then.

"See how you're freaking out right now?"

I growled.

"I'll take that as a yes." Another pet. "It sounds like their dad is sick and things at home are not so easy right now. Maybe they just wanted a nice little vacation and to be normal people for a spell."

I gave it some thought. Okay, that sounded kind of reasonable. And it did explain the part about them ditching their friends. Although these friends were likely some kind of official castle-type people. Wait, did people really live in castles anymore, or was I thinking of Disney World? Hmm. Sadie was actually making a ton more sense than I was.

But there were so many questions still. "You're sure these guys aren't in trouble or something? The CIA isn't after them?"

"Positive. As far as I can tell, all they've done since

they've been in the U.S. is go to a couple dinners and one of them played golf. Hardly a crime, except in the sense that golf is boring as shit." She grinned.

I took a breath and tried to take my mind back to the morning in my apartment. "So, let's say you're right, and they're just trying to keep a low profile and run wild for a couple days. What do we do?"

"That depends."

"On what?"

"On if you're okay hanging with them and helping out. I just thought you deserved to know." She gave me one last pat. "Well, that, and there was no possible way I could keep it to myself. I'm only human, after all."

I nodded absently as I thought. Did I want to throw in the towel and admit this was all too much? The thought of saying goodbye to Leo so soon made my chest hurt. And then I remembered the look on Malcolm's face this morning and his silly song in the shower. Ugh.

I thought for another minute and then sighed. "Okay."

"Okay, you're going to keep your plans? Or okay, you're done?"

"I'm gonna keep going. But for this to work, it means I can't let on that I know, doesn't it?" The thought of even more deceit made my stomach hurt.

Her smile was pained. "I think it's for the best. If they know you know, they'll be on guard the whole time, probably worried you'll somehow turn them in or call a reporter or something. I mean, I know you'd never do that, but they don't know you like I know you, you know?"

I shook my head to clear it, a bit impressed with myself

for following that. "True. Okay, so I need to somehow develop an awesome poker face in the next thirty seconds."

"Looks that way. I've been practicing mine all morning, but I think I'm just coming off as psycho instead."

That sparked a genuine laugh, one I really needed.

I took a deep breath and let it out as slowly as possible. "All right, then. I'm going on a road trip with two princes."

She nodded. "Yup. But first you have to get through lunch and pretend you haven't seen them half-naked." She opened the door for me. "And I'll need every detail of that later, by the way."

I cringed and followed Sadie back to the table.

Now that I knew who Leo and Malcolm really were, I expected them to look different somehow. But they appeared exactly the same as they had ten minutes earlier. Wind-tossed dark hair, those amazing cheekbones, super-hero t-shirts and jeans from Target. They didn't have an other-worldly glow and there was not a single crown in sight. Just the same two guys I'd been getting to know and like.

But they weren't really. Before I knew about their positions, they'd been regular people like Sadie and me, just with more money. Now they felt untouchable somehow. And even though I knew our time together was short-lived, I felt a bit ... cheated.

I went for the poker face, but by Leo's returning expression, I'd say it failed miserably. I leaned my crutches against the wall and immediately took my seat beside him so he wouldn't have such a clear view of my face.

"Are you okay?" He leaned into me and I could feel the

warmth of his breath on my cheek. I tried to suppress the memories it evoked.

I managed to lift the corners of my mouth a touch. "Fine. Sadie and I just had a couple things to talk about. Family stuff," I said, waving him off. He didn't need to know it was *his* family we'd been discussing.

I caught his short nod in my peripheral vision. "Ah." He sighed, although the sound was almost relieved. "I'm quite familiar with that."

"So!" Sadie dropped into the seat next to Malcolm. "What are you guys going to order?" From her level of enthusiasm, you'd think we were dining at freaking Spago and not a dive in Boone, North Carolina. Oh, God. They were probably used to gourmet everything and here we were offering them cheap burgers and onion straws. I hated this new discomfort and wished to God we were back in Stella cruising along the highway.

I looked over to see Malcolm studying me instead of his menu. I went for another smile but ended up biting my lip instead. His gaze shifted to Sadie who was practically bouncing in her seat and then returned to me again. I averted my eyes and forced myself to go for casual. "I'm getting a cheeseburger. I swear, the mountain air makes me starving."

Leo flipped his menu over. "I see they don't have lamb. A real shame."

I opened my mouth to apologize for the inferior selections when his meaning hit me. My mouth curved of its own accord this time and I spoke without thinking. "Serves you right for trying to eat something cute and fluffy. And I can tell you right now you won't be finding any baby Bessies in that kitchen either."

"Baby Bessies?" His lips twitched.

"Yeah. You know. Bessie. It's a classic cow name."

"No, it's not." His grin grew.

"Yes, it is. Right along with Elsie."

Malcolm choked on his drink from across the table. "That's our mother's name." He began coughing.

My heart started to thunder at the idea I just insulted a real live queen, but the sound of Leo's subsequent laughter acted like a cool river running through me. Before I knew it, I was laughing too. Leo's thigh pressed against mine and his arm went around me, as natural as can be. I looked across at Sadie and she pressed her lips together trying not to laugh and failing just like I had. For the moment, we were back to being two girls from Kernersville having lunch with a couple cute guys.

I decided then and there that I'd make this the best damn trip these boys had ever been on. And I wouldn't do it by tip-toeing around them. They wanted an authentic North Carolina experience? Well, I'd give it to them, my air-bag-free car, plain old cheeseburgers made from cows named Elsie, and everything in between.

"Oh, man. I wish I didn't have a test tomorrow or I'd totally come with you guys." We stood by Stella as Sadie hugged me goodbye.

I pulled back and pointed a finger at her. "You stay

focused. Only a few more weeks and you'll have that diploma in hand."

"Yes, ma'am." She gave me a mock salute and stepped back, making sure I was steady before releasing me entirely. Then, being Sadie, she went in for a hug with both brothers, even though she'd just met them and they were probably more used to curtseys than hugs from virtual strangers. But they didn't seem to mind.

Malcolm whispered something in her ear that had her snickering, and Sadie, in turn, whispered something to Leo as she embraced him. It was like a game of grade-school telephone and I was the kid with pink eye who wasn't allowed to play.

"What was that about?" I scowled at Malcolm as he took my crutches from me and opened the passenger door.

He winked. "Just having a little fun. No harm in that." He hopped over the side of the car and into the back as Leo extracted himself from Sadie's hug and got in the driver's seat.

"You do know the doors are here for a reason, right?" To which Malcolm just shrugged. But my attention had already transferred to Leo and I was trying to read his face, looking for clues as to what Sadie had told him. She was getting a strongly worded text, that was for damn sure.

"Bye!! Drive carefully and have fun!" Sadie shouted, waving her arms like crazy at us as we pulled out of the lot and rolled down the street. Her boho skirt billowed around her legs and her blond hair was wild. I blew her kisses and craned my neck until I could no longer see her. I wished I didn't have to leave her there, but I had a road trip to get on with.

"So, I hope nobody gets carsick, 'cuz we've got lots of twists and turns ahead." I pulled out my phone and opened the map. "I assume we're heading north?" Leo nodded and I prepared our route.

"May I see that for a minute?" Malcolm reached a hand over the seat and I could hear Leo groan in response. I chuckled and handed my phone over, but I knew which way to go so I directed Leo. And I didn't miss the little smiles he was sending my way. We were officially in flirtation mode, and despite my earlier discovery, I wasn't freaking the fuck out. Well, not much, at least.

"Here," Malcolm said after a couple minutes, tossing my phone up to me and making me fumble to catch it. He put an elbow on the top of each front bucket seat and brought his head almost level with ours. "Okay. New plan." I could have sworn I heard a whimper coming from Leo. "Fuck John Denver. The man couldn't even read a map. We need to go for true Americana. Something that makes people the world over say, "That's as American as it gets.""

"You want to go to Walmart?" I turned to face him.

"You do know we started this trip in the actual capital, right? White House? Smithsonian? Washington Monument? Any of this ringing a bell?" Leo threw in.

Malcolm dismissed both of us, his hands sweeping over our heads to form an imaginary marquee. "Coca-Cola." From the look on his face, I believe there was applause going off in his head.

Leo laughed in relief. "For a minute there, I thought you were going to suggest a side trip to Area 51." He shot Malcolm a quick glance. "Wait, forget I said that." When his brother didn't latch onto the alien plan, Leo continued,

"I'm pretty certain we can manage to buy you a Coke." He shifted gears and we sped up.

But Malcolm's head was already shaking. "No way. We're going to the source—the birthplace of the iconic American drink. We're going to Atlanta!"

I actually had to grab the steering wheel so Leo didn't crash Stella into a ditch.

LEO

Before we even got out of Boone, we stopped again. Mostly so I could wrap my head around Malcolm's latest ploy and Ruby could regain her confidence in my driving abilities. Malcolm, completely unbothered by my reaction, focused his efforts on convincing Ruby it was a terrific plan to change course to Atlanta. So we all sat soaking up the spring sun in a retail center car park in the mountains. Life could be worse.

Like his convenient obsession with John Denver, I knew this fascination with Coca-Cola was complete bollocks. Only one thing was clear—Malcolm was determined to create as much distance as possible between us and D.C.

When Ruby turned my way with apology in her eyes, I knew he'd gotten to her. I just had to remind myself that, despite what Malcolm may think, distance had no real impact on the eventual outcome of this endeavor. Planes flew out of Atlanta even more often than the capital. If he was surprised by my swift acquiescence, he didn't show it.

"We'll need to document the trip, of course," He said, jumping from the car and onto the pavement, drawing another warning noise from Ruby. "I don't know why I didn't think of it before." Mischief lit his face as he took off in a jog toward the mobile phone store occupying the end space on the chain of shops.

"You guys plan on burning through your entire stack of cash on this trip?" Ruby watched Malcolm as he entered the store and then turned her gray eyes to me.

"It really wouldn't be like Mal to scrimp." Honestly, I was shocked it had taken Ruby this long to reference our cashflow. But, even now, she was hardly scratching the surface with her flippant inquiry. It made me wonder again about her money situation. Perhaps her reluctance to question us too deeply had to do with a desire to keep her own cashflow issues to herself. But I wanted to help if I could.

"What about you? What are you going to spend your windfall on?"

She laughed, the sound sharp and decidedly unamused. She turned her phone in her hands. "Talk about a long and sordid story." Her eyes flashed to mine and she quickly added, "Maybe sordid is the wrong word. I mean," she stammered, "I'm not some dirtbag or something." Her brow furrowed adorably.

"The thought would never enter my mind." I turned my body to face her, wanting her to open up to me. A driving desire to gain her trust had my blood pumping faster. I steadfastly ignored the fact that I was an absolute hypocrite and was lying to her by omission. "Care to share? I'm an engineer. Troubleshooting is my life." I put a grave hand to my chest.

Ruby's eyes traveled around the car park, following a family as they made their way into a deli. When her gaze finally came back to me, I tried not to look too eager. One side of her mouth curved upward. "I don't think my problems are the kind you can fix with math and brainpower. No offense." She forced her smile to grow, but I could tell it was only for my benefit. "And, anyway, this trip is about you guys. And, believe me, ten thousand dollars is a dream come true! I would feel guilty taking it, but my guess is your brother spends as much on lunch." She glanced back at the phone shop.

I couldn't help but press again. "Are you sure you don't want to tell me?"

"I wouldn't want to damage your delicate sensibilities." Genuine amusement crossed her face this time.

I pulled the imaginary knife from my chest. "Ouch. I'll have you know I've dealt with some pretty serious stuff. Way more scandalous than anything you could be embroiled in."

She looked like she almost believed me. Her head began to shake, but I saw the moment she changed her mind. Then she shifted so we were both sideways in our seats, face to face. Her black t-shirt stretched across her breasts and one of those long legs folded under her, making me momentarily forget what we were talking about. I wanted to smooth my hand over her thigh and kiss the area around her wounds. This had the potential to be awkward.

"You asked for it. Get ready to be shocked."

I straightened my spine and rolled my shoulders before giving her a bring-it-on gesture. She laughed. "I don't think I've ever met anyone like you, Leo Baxter." Her eyes traced my features and I had to hold myself back from leaning over to kiss her. But this was about her, not my body's desire to rub up against her naked.

"Right back at you, Ruby ..." My head jerked back. "I just realized I don't know your last name." Hmm. The sound of Trevor succumbing to heart failure a hundred miles east of us echoed faintly in my ears.

"Green."

"Wait, your name is Ruby Green?"

"I know. You don't need to say it."

"Well, it could be Red," I offered weakly.

"I believe I'd spontaneously morph into a cartoon character if that were the case."

"Okay, Ruby Green, I'm all ears." Before I realized what I was doing, I reached out for her hand. She didn't pull it back, so I held onto it, feeling the roughened callouses on the pads of her fingers and wondering why the sensation of them against my own skin felt better than even the palace's highest thread-count sheets. She took a breath and I squeezed her hand in encouragement.

"Okay, so, you've met Sadie." This didn't require a reply so I made no sound. "Right. Anyway, she's amazing." Her pink lips spread in a wide grin. "We grew up together —literally. I lived with my aunt and uncle for most of my childhood and Sadie's always been like a little sister to me."

Sadie was lovely. She was sweet and exuberant, and quite pretty. I was assuming there was much more to the story since her cousin seemed the furthest thing from problematic. And then Ruby continued.

"She has a brother." Her smile morphed into a lip curl. Ah. "Jason is between Sadie and me in age, but we never got along. I'm not sure why—I think it had something to do with him resenting the attention I got from his parents."

She rubbed her nose as she thought about it, and it was cute as hell. "His dad is the one I run the auto shop with. Carl. He's my mom's brother, and he and Aunt Beth were more like parents to me than my own were. When Carl saw I had an interest in cars, he kind of took me under his wing and everything just clicked, you know? He's the one who gave me Stella for my twenty-first birthday. She was a huge mess, but I loved her anyway." Her eyes were bright.

I nodded and ran my thumb over the back of her hand as she continued. "Jason had always been getting into some kind of trouble or other, but that was when he ramped it up. He started getting busted for vandalism and smoking dope. Nothing too serious, but a far cry from model behavior, that's for sure." She stopped and looked up at me again with those eyes. "Are you sure you want to hear all this? It's probably boring you half to death—or scaring you."

"Not at all. You haven't heard my stories about Malcolm yet." I cringed.

That made her smile and she resumed her story. "Anyway, when Carl offered me the partnership with the shop a couple years back, Jason lost his shit. Which was ridiculous since he'd never shown an interest in working on cars—just driving them too fast. He and Carl had this big blow-out and Jason took off. We didn't hear from him for two months." This Jason guy sounded like a right prick.

"As awful luck would have it, that was the same time we found out Beth had stage-four breast cancer. Carl was a mess, and Sadie and I did everything we could to find Jason. We figured he'd just fall deeper down whatever hole he was in if his mom died and he hadn't even known she was sick."

Ruby paused and blinked, probably lost in the memories. "Sorry." Her lips formed a self-conscious half smile. "Long story short, we found him and he at least got to say goodbye to Beth before she passed, but he was caught up with these really nasty pieces of work by that point, and he was acting like more of an asshole than ever. Sadie and Carl and I basically had to let him go do his thing while we all grieved. It was a really awful time." Her head shook and she played with her phone again.

I squeezed her hand, wishing I could go back in time and take some of that pain away, but all I could do was listen.

"So, fast forward eighteen months and Carl gets a call from Jason in the middle of the night. He's been arrested for armed robbery. Needless to say, Carl flipped his shit. But Jason, the douchebag that he is, played right into Carl's sense of family and regret and the next thing we knew, Carl put the garage up as collateral and bailed Jason out."

Shit. This did not sound good.

Her mouth twisted. "At this point, I feel I must note that Jason, to this day, has never even thanked Carl." I hoped my face reflected how much I'd like to kick this guy's arse.

"Anyway, a lawyer was appointed, hearings were scheduled, blah, blah, blah. Only, there's a reason Sadie's the one in college and not Jason. Besides being a complete jerk, he's also dumb as a box of rocks. In other words, the guy is no criminal mastermind." Ruby's hand waved in the air. "There were prints, witnesses, the whole shebang. And idiot though he may be, even he saw the writing on the wall. He was due for his last court date about a week ago and, POOF, he disappeared. No sign of him anywhere."

Shit.

I leaned forward so she'd look up at me again. "Which means the bail is forfeited, I assume?"

She met my eyes. "You got it in one." Her voice was quiet.

"And the auto shop?" And her apartment?

Her head shook with vehemence. "Nope. Not gonna happen. I already told Carl we're not losing the garage. I've got feelers out to find Jason." Her face softened. "And now I have ten thousand bucks toward the cause, thanks to two dirty hitchhikers I picked up on the side of the road." She grinned.

I couldn't believe she could smile in the midst of everything she was going through. She shouldn't be carting our spoiled butts around the countryside because Malcolm was avoiding being crowned a bloody king. I was embarrassed for us. Yet Ruby smiled. And my chest got even tighter.

"I think I really need to kiss you right now."

Ruby's mouth popped open, forming a perfect O and making me want to pull her onto my lap. "Um. Okay."

There was no hesitating this time. I closed the space between us and captured her mouth with mine. Her skin was warm from the sun and her lips tasted sweet as I drew their flavor into my mouth. I used one hand to brace myself on the seat and the other dove into her hair, loosening some strands the wind had missed. It was silk and so was her skin. I slid my tongue out to swipe her upper lip and she opened for me, making me groan and press in. There was a tether in our connection that pulled at my gut and groin, turning me on and speeding the rush of blood through my entire body.

It was like our contact that morning, but a thousand times more intense. Her arms wound around me, one hand sliding across my shoulder blades while the other gripped the back of my neck. Her tongue was soft and wet as it danced against mine, tasting, exploring, hungry for more. I leaned back, pulling her with me so my hand didn't have to support us any longer and I was free to trace her body with my fingers and palms. I wanted nothing more than to keep her body draped over me, preferably naked, for the foreseeable future.

Ruby tilted her head and renewed her efforts to drive me crazy with her tongue and lips. My back hit the driver's side door and my hands slid to her lower back, one traveling down to her hip and then the back of her thigh where bare skin met the pads of my fingers. Christ, I could feel my cock clamoring, and Ruby wasn't doing anything but encouraging it by rubbing herself on top of me.

Just as I was about to get my first feel of her incredible backside, the most annoying sound in the universe blared from the passenger seat.

You know the one—Dah-dah-dun-dun-dun, dah-dah-dun-dun-dun—over and over in that pitch that makes you want to go back to the days of rotary phones.

Ruby pulled back on a sharp inhale, her head swinging

from side to side as if to orient herself. Both of us blinked in the bright light of the afternoon. Ruby bent to snatch her phone and silence the awful ringing. My hope was we'd get right back to business, but the look on her face as she stared at the screen said otherwise.

As did the look on Malcolm's face as he lowered his new phone and tapped a button. "Now *that's* what I call prime holiday footage."

"Hand that over, you prick!" I reached out and tried to snatch the phone from his hands, but he was too quick.

"Don't worry. I'll send you a copy when we're back on the grid."

I looked to Ruby to see exactly how close she was to murdering my brother, but her lip was caught between her teeth and her eyes hadn't left her own phone. Well, this couldn't be good.

Ruby was quiet as we finally turned onto the Blue Ridge Parkway and headed southwest for Asheville. She'd not been wrong. The scenery was spectacular and the road was one winding curve after another. Most of the Feldlands was flat as a griddlecake, which made it perfect for windmills, but not as ideal for scenery. The mountains were a revelation.

But I was distracted by Ruby. I wanted desperately to know who'd called her and what she was thinking. I wasn't about to bring it up in Malcolm's presence, though. The story was hers to share if she so chose. And I'd get her alone later to ask about it. Both the call and her thoughts undoubtedly had to do with her family, and I'd do what I could to help, especially if it put a smile back on her face.

By the time we reached the outskirts of Asheville, Malcolm was looking more than a little green. The Parkway had lost some of its charm and managed to achieve what a liter of liquor couldn't. While he expelled the contents of his stomach in a roadside bush, Ruby tapped into her phone looking for lodging options and wincing every time Malcolm's retching reached our ears. We still hadn't told her we couldn't use credit cards. I'd leave it to Mal to figure that one out. He was the master of bullshit, after all. But this would be yet another lie to pile on top of the stack sitting between us. Frustration didn't begin to describe my feelings on that.

Malcolm stumbled back to the Mustang.

"Do not get in here if you're not done puking." Ruby's eyes didn't even lift from her phone.

Mal leaned against the car, inhaling slowly. "You're a regular Florence Nightingale, aren't you? I'll bet you wouldn't be so heartless to Leo."

That brought her eyes to him, her head tilting to see him better. "That's because Leo is a decent human being and is not holding video of my ass hostage. He also has excellent manners."

Malcolm scowled at me and crossed his arms, letting out a belch I wouldn't trust from five meters away. Ruby pointed to the bushes.

"*I'm* the one who has respect for Stella, not Leo! He thinks she's a curse to the planet!"

Ruby swung her head around to me and my hands went up in defense. "I never said that."

"But you thought it!" I continued to shake my head as Malcolm went on. "And I'm giving you ten thousand dollars. From my own personal bank account!"

Ruby turned back to him. "Yeah, about that. I'm getting the impression there's enough in that account that you won't miss it much."

"That's neither here nor there." He paused and held a finger up, his face losing color, and then sprinted back to the bushes.

"So, maybe we should call it a day and stop for the night," Ruby suggested, her expression one of distaste. Not that I blamed her.

"Uh, yeah. Sure." My response was less than convincing.

"Everything okay?" Ruby set her phone in her lap and turned all her attention to me.

Bugger. Damn Malcolm. "Uh, yeah. It's just ... do you know if any places around here take cash?"

This was the moment ninety-nine percent of people would lose their patience with us and demand to know what in the hell was going on. But not Ruby. She took in my question with no change in expression and let it sit between us for a moment.

"So, no credit or debit card?"

I slowly shook my head, bracing once again.

Her eyes narrowed, but not at me—more like she was performing complicated mathematics in her head. I held my breath until she raised a finger and then started typing into her phone again.

Malcolm returned, looking slightly better. "I am in desperate need of a shower and a toothbrush. But I can safely say there is nothing left in here." He pointed to his gut.

It took another ten minutes before Ruby felt confident enough to allow Malcolm re-entry. By this time, she had found what she was looking for on her phone and directed me through several turns before we came to a modest-looking motor inn with a name I'd not heard before. The place was not nearly as frightening as some I'd seen along the way, but still dodgy enough that I wouldn't be bringing a black light in with me. I applied the parking break in front of the glass-doored office and Ruby held an upturned palm out to me. I was about to take her hand in my own when she said, "I'll need some cash."

I'd sort of assumed she was planning on using her own credit card and we'd pay her the cash in exchange, but I may have been wrong. In fact, it was possible she didn't have a credit card at all. I handed her three hundred dollars, prompting Malcolm to grunt in disgust from the backseat and slap another five hundred in her hand.

Ruby opened her door and hoisted herself out, testing her weight on her ankle.

"Why don't you let me handle it?" I asked.

She shook her head and bent to look at herself in the side mirror. She smoothed her eyebrows and pinched her cheeks before standing upright again and tying the hem of her t-shirt in a knot, exposing a few inches of creamy skin at her waist. I moved to get out, but her look stopped me in my seat. Mal put a staying hand on my shoulder.

Ruby winked at me and then began walking with only the slightest limp.

"At least take your crutches!" I shouted, but she just

threw me a wave without turning back. She had to be in a lot of pain. I had a good idea what she was doing, but that didn't make it any easier to watch.

She disappeared inside and I may have growled. "Down, boy," Mal said, patting my shoulder.

Ten minutes later, Ruby collapsed in the passenger seat again, holding out one key to me and grasping another in her other hand. "We're the last two rooms on the end." She pointed to the other side of the building. "And Russell invited us to join him for a private screening of Weird Science later tonight. I don't want to get your hopes up, Malcolm, but I believe there was a coded reference to moonshine as well."

Malcolm whimpered from the backseat and I drove us down to claim our rooms. The fact that I neglected to pick up a burner phone or find a way to contact Trevor was pushed to the back of my mind as memories of Ruby's mouth on mine consumed the majority of my available headspace.

CHAPTER FOURTEEN

RUBY

Three things were clear. (1) Leo Baxter kissed like he'd been training for it his entire life; (2) I needed some time in the shower to replay our too-brief make-out session and clean the road dirt off me; and (3) Nash wasn't going to let me enjoy either of the first two. Damn the man.

Leo, gentleman that he was, helped me into my room and carried my bag before shooting me a meaningful "this isn't over" look and closing the door behind him. All sorts of tingly sensations gathered in various parts of my body, but I couldn't give them my full attention.

I'd been purposely avoiding the fact that I owed Nash a phone call, and it seemed his patience had run out. I abandoned the crutches on the spare bed and sat on the orange floral coverlet of the other. I pulled out my phone and held my breath as I listened to Nash's voicemail.

"Ru-by." He stretched my name out in a way that had any remaining Leo tingles flying to the wind. "Word is you struck out at Benny's last night. You gotta find a way to avoid Trish. You should know better. I expect a report in the morning, but not too early. I got plans tonight—you're welcome to join when you're done at Benny's. You just let me know." I could hear the smarmy curve of his lips. "Starting to get a line on your boy, so I shouldn't need to remind you I'll be collecting payment in one form or another. Later."

I immediately hit delete and prioritized that shower. Dammit. This wasn't going to be as easy to back out of as I thought. I considered calling Nash right away and telling him to stop his search, but I only had the first five thousand at the moment and that wasn't going to get me very far. I'd wait until I had all ten and then figure out a way to get him to back off. Then I'd sell Stella and we'd have the money if the police didn't find Jason in time.

A knock drew my attention, but it wasn't coming from the door. I looked around the outdated but tidy space and saw that there was one of those doors to an adjoining room. I limped over and unlocked my side, then swung the door open.

The sound of a shower running had me impatient for my own, but it could wait until I got to enjoy Leo standing in my doorway looking like he had all sorts of ideas floating around in that handsome head of his. I couldn't help the smile forming on my lips. Nash who?

"So, are you going to tell me about your conversation with Russell?" He was grinning at me, but there was that little V between his brows.

I outright laughed at this. "Russell is a simple man. A bit of cash, a hint of boob, and we were fast friends." This, of course, brought his eyes down to my rack and my girls weren't unaffected.

Leo ran a hand through his hair, making it even messier and tempting my hands to comb through it. His expression was a mix of lust and frustration, and I have to admit I enjoyed it. He glanced back at the bathroom where Malcolm was clearly showering.

"When Malcolm gets done we can figure out dinner. I'm heading down to the office to see if there's a laundry facility. I'm not looking forward to wearing these same clothes—or the ones from yesterday."

I wasn't fooled, and I let the smile linger on my lips. He was going to stake his claim with Russell. The same Russell who undoubtedly owned every piece of Star Trek memorabilia ever made and probably still lived with his mother.

A thought occurred to me. "Hey, are you going to tell me what Sadie said to you in the parking lot?"

His eyes went to my lips as his own quirked. "Maybe after I check on laundry."

I rolled my eyes and shut the door in his face. "I'm taking a shower!"

I heard a half-laugh, half-groan. This was fun.

It took two rounds of conditioner to get the wind-blown tangles from my hair. The hot water ran down my hair and back, drawing a sigh from my lungs. I took the soap in my hands and began lathering up, letting my lips tilt up as I remembered Leo's face in the doorway and then Leo's hands as they moved over me in the car. I'd completely forgotten we were out in public when he pulled me over him. All I could think of was the taste of his lips and the feel of his hands on my skin. Both then and now.

My right hand slid from my neck, down to my breast where my nipple hardened under my fingers. I closed my eyes and blindly set the soap aside as my other hand ran over my stomach and down between my legs. I slid my middle finger between my lower lips and found my clit, stroking it as I imagined Leo's hand there. It didn't take long before my heart rate quickened along with my strokes. I pinched one nipple and then the other, letting out a moan as I pictured Leo's mouth on my breasts and his own sounds of appreciation. My finger circled and pressed over and over until I felt the rush of my orgasm approaching. I considered trying to hold it off, but I was too far gone. I moaned loudly and it echoed with the shower's acoustics, but I didn't care. Shudders overtook me and my right hand went to the wall to steady me as I rode out my climax. Damn, Leo was amazing, even when he wasn't in the same room.

My breathing came in pants as I recovered from my orgasm and finally opened my eyes. I was back in the dingy shower in an old motel, all by myself. I sighed and finished cleaning myself before turning off the water and wrapping one towel around my hair and one around my body. I wasn't usually one for one-night-stands and affairs that had no potential to go anywhere, but I was seriously considering making an exception for Leo. And, besides, he was a prince, so there was that. I let out a small laugh, still unable to fully process that fact. It was all too bizarre.

The mirror was covered in condensation, so I opened the bathroom door, my smile remaining.

Standing immediately outside the door was the very same prince I'd just had on my dirty mind. Every muscle in his body was coiled like a snake ready to strike. I yelped and almost fell when I instinctively put a foot back. The doorway anchored me and my eyes flew to Leo's. If any part of me was in doubt that he knew exactly what I was doing in that shower, one look at his barely-there irises cleared up the matter. His eyes were liquid with lust and, damn, I was already holding up that white flag of surrender.

He moved like that snake and yanked me forward, covering my mouth with his and pressing my back against the wall beside the bathroom door. His tongue invaded my mouth, stroking and tasting every last spot. I quickly caught up once I got over my shock. My hands were in his hair, my tongue and lips eagerly joining in the duel with his. Damn, the boy smelled good. He was fresh air, clean sweat, spice, and something distinctly Leo.

He pulled the towel from my hair, his hands tangling in the wet strands and moving my head to the exact angle he wanted. It was HOT. Then one of his hands dropped and ran down my towel-covered body until it reached the thigh of my injured leg. He pulled it up, my knee bending as he pressed the hard evidence of his arousal between my legs. I didn't care one bit that my towel was coming apart in the middle. It felt too damn good to give one thought to modesty. Or anything, for that matter, that wasn't getting our skin in immediate naked contact with one another.

Leo groaned into my mouth and then his lips were gone. I opened my eyes to see that he'd dropped to his knees, my bent leg now resting on his shoulder as he used one hand to yank the towel from around me. Hot damn! This boy had gone and lost his Emily Post stamp of approval, and I couldn't be happier about it. My breathing was ragged as he lifted his eyes to my face in silent question. I just blindly put a hand to his hair and tilted my head back where it thunked against the wall as the first touch of Leo's fingers to my already-swollen flesh sent sparks flying through me.

As if that wasn't enough to send me into a sensual tizzy, the feel of his wet, hot tongue on my sensitive clit almost made me orgasm right then and there. I felt the vibration of his moan as he lapped at my bundle of nerves and slick skin. I honestly didn't know if I could go on without falling into a heap on the floor. My one knee wasn't doing a very good job of keeping me upright. But Leo's hold on me tightened as he used one hand to support me while his other held me open to him. It was magic. I was getting close and I knew I was moaning and whimpering as his tongue continued to move and stroke. And then I was bucking over his face and pulling his hair as I shouted my climax and his movements picked up speed, encouraging my orgasm to stretch out as long as possible. He only pulled back when the aftershocks slowed and I was able to mostly support myself. He leaned back on his heels, his hands holding onto my hips as his face tilted up to me again. His cheeks were flushed and his eyes smoky.

"Fuck," was all he said.

I couldn't form any words at all yet. Not even one as simple as that.

Loud and insistent knocking on the adjoining door had

both our heads whipping to the side. I breathed a sigh of relief that it was at least closed.

"I just wanted you horny little bastards to know these walls are not soundproof! I repeat, these walls are *not* soundproof! In other news, well done, Leo!"

My head hit the wall again, this time most definitely not in response to the sexy man at my feet.

I glared across the table at Malcolm who had yet to wipe the smug grin from his face since he'd interrupted Leo and me at the motel. He obviously had zero understanding of how to get in a woman's good graces. Leo's thumb rubbed the side of my thigh as his hand rested on my leg. He hadn't stopped touching me since our hot motel-room connection, apart from the time he'd taken to have his own shower. I was only too happy to run all our laundry down to the coin operated-machines Leo had discovered on his earlier quest. After all, I was the only one with a bag of clean clothes to wear, and it was much better than sticking around tolerating Malcolm's commentary on Leo and me. That, and the sight of him walking around shamelessly in his boxers.

Leo must have had a talk with him because he wasn't saying one word about it when I returned from the laundry room, and he'd also positioned himself under the sheets of one of the beds. That didn't stop all the meaningful looks and that damn grin, though. Good God, that boy needed a hobby.

We sat and watched an Avengers movie for a bit until the dryer cycle finished and the Baxter brothers got dressed in clean clothes for a late dinner. We drove into town and I took them to Avenue M where we ordered the best fettuccine on earth and I fully planned to let Malcolm pay the bill. Served him right. Sadie and I had been to the restaurant on a trip to Asheville with Aunt Beth a few years earlier, and the memory warmed me. Until Malcolm's stupid face brought me back. How two identical faces could conjure such opposing reactions was a true wonder.

I was somewhat grateful that Leo and I hadn't gotten any alone time since his trip, *ahem*, downtown. Not that I didn't want a repeat as well as a more extensive exploration of this thing between us, but I needed to catch my breath and make sure I had my head on straight. We had maybe one or two more days and then we'd never see each other again. I had to let that sink in before I threw caution to the wind.

Leo had the power to be all-consuming. I could feel it. He had this kind of stealthy charisma. You don't see it coming with his nice manners and dry humor and then BAM—Prince Charm-Your-Panties-Off is suddenly gazing at you from the next pillow over and you've just been thoroughly laid.

The bottom line was I didn't want regrets, either way things went. But I also didn't want to be nursing a broken heart in two days' time.

Leo and Malcolm were talking about someone named Alice who I gathered worked for Malcolm.

"Is Alice one of the friends you guys ditched?" I took a sip of my beer and ignored the look that passed between the brothers. It was clear they were deliberating how much to share with me. I didn't feel like making it easy on

Malcolm. "By the way, what do you do for a living, anyway, Malcolm? I know Leo's an engineer, but you haven't talked about your job."

Leo leaned an elbow on the table and rested his chin in his hand, a sly smile overtaking his mouth. "Yes, Malcolm, what *is* it you do?"

Malcolm cleared his throat and wiped his mouth with a cloth napkin. He eyed me carefully, but I just smiled. This should be good. "I'm, uh, between jobs at the moment."

Leo covered his mouth and I pretended to consider Malcolm's statement. "Hmm. So, what did you study at school?"

Malcolm waved a hand in the air. "Oh, you know, a bit of this, a bit of that." His gaze swept the restaurant, undoubtedly in search of our waitress to come save his ass.

"I see. I'm assuming you went to college with Leo. What was *your* major?"

Leo cut in. "I believe it was political science, wasn't it? No, wait. Religious studies?"

"Christ, no," Malcolm scowled. Then he turned to me. "As Leo well knows, I dropped out in my first year. I had other things that needed my attention."

Leo turned to me. "What he means is women, cars, and liquor."

I decided to give Malcolm a break. "Well, I can't fault you for the car thing. My version of college was working on cars under the guidance of my uncle. College would have been a waste of money we didn't have anyway." I shrugged.

Another look passed between the brothers and I wanted to roll my eyes. "Before you even start thinking of feeling bad for me, my career is a dream come true. *I feel* bad for people who have to work doing something they hate just to bring home a big paycheck." Although that big paycheck sure would come in handy for the Jason bullshit, I didn't normally consider it.

Malcolm just looked at the table and Leo sent a forced smile my direction. What had I said?

The waitress brought the check and I didn't even have the heart to joke around as Malcolm pulled out a few bills and handed it back. Leo squeezed my leg.

"So, what's your next restoration project after Stella?" Leo asked, changing the subject. But Malcolm never looked up or engaged in more conversation. I almost missed the smug smile. Almost.

CHAPTER FIFTEEN

LEO

There was no way for Ruby to know her comment about careers would hit so close to home for Malcolm. As I've admitted, I sort of enjoy it when he gets knocked off his golden, ne'er-do-well high horse once in a while. It's good for him, after all. But time was flying, and our father would be stepping down in a matter of weeks. Things were getting a bit too real.

Mal slipped into our room as soon as we returned to the motel, but I lingered outside Ruby's room. I knew she hadn't missed his change in mood.

"I'm sorry if I said something to upset Malcolm at dinner," she said, leaning against the door jamb. "I mean, apart from generally giving him the hard time I'm entitled to." I thought she might blush at the reference to Malcolm's earlier interruption, but she didn't. The only thing I got was a naughty grin, and I liked it a whole lot.

A single lamplight buzzed near us and I shook my head. "No. You didn't do anything wrong. He's just got some changes coming up when we get home, and he's not really looking forward to it."

She looked to the ground and her Converse-clad feet for a few moments. "So, the between-jobs thing?"

"Yeah." I scratched my stubbled jaw and moved to lean against the other side of the doorway. "He's got a new ... job lined up and it comes with a lot of responsibility. As you can imagine, he's not too keen on that." I let myself grin, but I truly did feel for my brother. Not that I could share all the details with Ruby, even though I wanted nothing more. Especially considering the level of intimacy we'd shared. This situation was less than ideal, to put it mildly.

The sound of the television switching on had us both glancing toward the room Malcolm and I were sharing.

"Do you think you should go talk to him?" I looked back to find Ruby examining my features in the dim light.

It pained me, but I nodded. What I really wanted to do was pull Ruby to me and do all the things my imagination had been conjuring for the last twenty-four hours. "I should. He may come off as a carefree lay-about, but this one is hitting him hard." I felt like I owed her a better expla-nation, but all I said was, "It's complicated."

She reached out and grabbed my hand. I turned it in mine and brought it to my mouth, kissing the pulse point at her wrist and pulling her closer in the process. Her eyes went liquid and I could see a shiver of awareness run through her body. Just the sight of that and the feel of her skin under my lips had my cock hardening. "I can still taste you on my tongue," I whispered.

Her eyes widened for a second and then she leaned in and placed an all-too-brief kiss on my mouth. "I'll be up for a while yet if you and Malcolm finish talking things out." Then she crossed the threshold into her room and shut the door, not breaking eye contact until it closed completely.

I was a dead man. This woman was slowly killing me with her fiery spirit and sexy mouth.

Since neither Malcolm nor I would appreciate my cock entering the room before the rest of me, I counted backward from one hundred and forced my thoughts to Vladimir Putin. It took a minute, but it eventually worked and I went in to check on my brother. He was a rather pathetic sight, sprawled in a giant X over the dull orange bedcovers, his head propped on one lonely pillow and his neck straining to give him a view of the travel program playing on the television. I perched myself on the other bed and faced him, my elbows to my knees. He finally looked my way.

"Planning a trip to Costa Rica, are you?"

He shrugged. "Wouldn't mind it."

I chewed my lip and his eyes returned to the screen. "Want to talk about it?"

"I think with some safety precautions, it could work. They say you have to be alert for pick-pockets and scammers, though."

I grinned at his deliberate misunderstanding of my question. At least his sense of humor was still intact. "I'll make a note of that."

He turned his eyes to me again. "Don't worry about me,

Leo. I'm just having a small pity party for one. Go enjoy a night with Ruby." He gestured to the adjoining room. "I'll even turn the volume up so I can't hear you." He attempted a grin but it fell flat.

I readjusted myself on the bed, leaning back and propping two pillows under my head. "Maybe in a bit. I'm developing a new fascination with scam artists in Costa Rica right now."

We fell silent and watched the footage of a bustling San Jose, lush rainforests, and vacationers sunning on beaches.

"It isn't as if any of us wants this. That's the worst part, I think," Malcolm finally spoke.

I grunted my agreement. He was one-hundred percent right. We all knew Malcolm would succeed to the throne at some point, but it was meant to be when he was much older. Our father was only fifty-eight and had no desire to step down. But illness often doesn't pay heed to age or the wishes of the rest of us. And it had come for the king of the Feldlands. Not that he was dying, thank God, but his multiple sclerosis had begun to ravish him in the past year, making the situation a difficult one at best. As long as he was mentally acute, there was no need for King Gregory to step down, but then an incident occurred a few months back that changed the picture.

His multiple sclerosis was no secret, and to this point, he'd been a virtual billboard for people with disabilities' rights to equal treatment in the workplace. The fact that his workplace was a palace didn't seem to matter much. People respected him for it and loved him even more for it. But in February, he was delivering a speech and completely lost his place. It was as if the words simply vanished. Our father, the king of our small nation, stood silently before an audience of thousands and couldn't speak a word. To this day, I'm not sure which was worse, the lost look on his face or the utter silence itself.

Of course, the media went mad, making all manner of assumptions. The facts no longer mattered. Our father was as intelligent as ever, but the disease had progressed past the physical and into the cognitive, affecting his short-term memory and his ability to, as he put it, "find my bloody words!" Countless meetings were called, strategies born, and options offered. But the damage had been done. If the public doubted the mental ability of its leaders, it was time for a change. Fighting it would only put off the inevitable and create a divisive atmosphere in the process.

It was finally our mother, the Queen, who put an end to further discussion. She is loyal to two things: family and country, and very much in that order, although at times the implications of that may appear otherwise. The Queen's word is law, whether that be in a political arena or the vegetable garden outside the palace kitchens. Our father would step down and Malcolm would take the throne. Ready or not. Willing or not. Qualified or not.

But Malcolm *was* qualified. As much as he pretended not to exercise his intellect in situations involving business and society, it was just a game. All of us, even Malcolm, knew that Queen Elsie would never risk besmirching the family name by allowing an unqualified heir to take the throne. Although evidence may suggest otherwise, she had faith in Malcolm. And so did I. Malcolm was the one who needed to find belief in himself, and he'd have to do that on his own. But I would always be there to encourage him. We all would.

I repositioned the pillows under my head. "Remember the time Father caught me disassembling the Charles II clock in his office at Gelhurst? I thought he was having a heart attack with how bloody furious he was."

"Vaguely. What was your punishment that time? No Science Channel for two weeks? Good lord, you were a boffin—still are."

I let it slide, both because this was about him, not me, and because he was right. "No, I didn't get punished at all."

I heard his hand hit the bed. "Unbelievable! I would have been banished to my room for at least two weeks. That clock was a priceless heirloom!"

"I know."

"Why aren't they making *you* king again?"

I crossed my arms over my chest. "Because you told Father that you'd asked me how clocks work, and before he could protest, you went on to explain how allowing children to conduct hands-on experiments leads to elevated problem-solving abilities, critical thinking, and memory retention. Then you said he'd regret suppressing my curious nature at such a young age and I'd likely end up a factory worker instead of an inventor of groundbreaking technology."

Malcolm propped himself up on two elbows and eyed me over the table separating us. "I said that?"

I nodded. "You did. I'll never forget it. It was the single best piece of bullshit I'd heard in my life to that date."

He nodded, considering that. "It does sound bloody brilliant, though." Then his chin jerked to me. "And, hey! It turned out to be true. Look at you and your high-tech solutions. Well done, me!"

I chuckled at him, glad to see the ego back in place. "Yes, well done, you."

"Do you think Father actually believed all that?"

I shook my head. "Not a fucking word. But you were so quick with it." I snapped my fingers. "Just like that. You dove in to defend me, and you talked your way around the thing until you had everyone listening, considering a different view."

Malcolm made a noise and laid back down.

"Not bad for a twelve-year-old. Just think what that kid could do now." I paused, hoping my words would sink in.

A pillow sailed over the table and hit me in the face. "Nice try, arsehole."

I barked out a laugh but didn't respond. Because every word I said was true.

Thirty minutes and two countries later, Malcolm switched off the television and stood from the bed. His arms stretched above his head and he rocked his neck from side to side as if preparing for some daring physical endeavor. "Well, the time has come."

Having not a single clue what he was on about, I just raised a brow.

"I'm getting my first taste of moonshine, my friend. This Russell person is about to become the future king's best mate."

I snorted and shook my head at him, sitting up on the bed. "Do you require a designated walker?"

"No. I'll manage. But you have your own friends to make." He jerked his chin to the next room over. "I like to refer to them as Kylie and Kendall." He pointed to each of his nipples in turn.

If I growled at him in response, it was only because killing him wasn't really an option.

He laughed and sidestepped my hand as it went for the back of his head. It was nice to see his good mood restored, though.

"Now, go forth and conquer, my brother. And, please, do absolutely *everything* I would do." With that, he was out the door.

I checked my watch. It was past midnight and I had no idea if Ruby was still awake. I went to the sink and brushed my teeth. Then I came back out and paced in front of the adjoining door. I put my ear to it but couldn't hear anything coming from her room. Bugger. I paced some more and then went back to the mirror to make sure I didn't have anything on my face. I smelled my shirt, checking that it hadn't absorbed any restaurant smells like garlic or something fishy. No, it was fine. More pacing.

I jumped back when the door swung open and Ruby stood just inside her room, a tiny smirk on her face, and from what I could tell, just a pink t-shirt covering her body.

"I can hear you lumbering around in here like a buffalo. What in the hell are you doing?"

Oh. I guess she was up.

"Sorry. Did I wake you?"

"No." Her mirth was poorly contained.

"Good." I put my hands in my pockets and rocked on my heels. I was acting like a bloody moron.

Her smile widened and she pulled on my arm. "Come on, Casanova."

I allowed her to drag me into her room and closed the door behind me.

There had been no forethought—other than my general feelings of lust toward her—to our earlier episode. Pure carnal instinct had led us. But this was different. I found myself giving it careful thought, wanting to make everything perfect, maybe so I could hold onto this one flawless moment when we parted ways. Whatever it was, it had me acting like a virgin schoolboy. This wouldn't do at all. I took a breath and gave myself the mental beating I needed. There was no way I was cocking this up—except in the most literal sense.

By the time Ruby turned around again, I had my wits about me and her amused grin dropped at the new expression I wore. I was going for, "Prepare yourself to be utterly ravaged," and all signs indicated I'd succeeded. She even gave a little gasp before I took her mouth.

CHAPTER SIXTEEN

RUBY

Mister Awkward had officially left the building and Prince Charm-Your-Panties-Off was back and getting down to business.

I'd been going back and forth in my mind about how far I wanted to take things with Leo, but I eventually decided to go with the horny part of my brain that rationalized he'd already been all up in my lady bits, so I may as well check out the other ways Leo Baxter could rock my world.

He was off to a killer start. His warm, demanding lips collided with mine and I didn't hesitate to wrap both arms around him and pull him in. He was back to the white t-shirt and jeans and his feet were bare, a small detail that I found both adorable and sexy. I never really thought I had a type, apart from my misguided foray into bad-boy land, but Leo's whole sexy-nerd thing was doing it for me big time.

His tongue swept past my lips and into my mouth, tasting as he went, his groan of pleasure running through me. I stroked my tongue against his and made like a cat, clawing at his back and rubbing up against him, trying to come into contact with every part of him at once. This was *so* happening. I moved back, pulling him with me toward the bed but his mouth suddenly broke contact, making me blink in surprise.

"Wait." His eyes were lust-drunk, so I didn't understand.

"Wh-what?" I managed.

"Where is your phone?" He pulled his hands from me, leaving my skin cold where his touch had just been.

WTF?

I pointed hesitantly to the bedside table. Who in the hell did he need to call at this precise moment?! We had boobs and hot kisses and a sizable erection from what I'd been able to glean thus far, so what was the holdup? Was there some royal rule about asking permission before doing the deed? *Excuse me, Your Majesty, but I'd like to engage in hot, sweaty fornication with a horny girl from North Carolina. What say you?*

I watched as Leo snatched the phone from the table and strode to the doors connecting our rooms. Was he leaving?! He opened my side and then executed an underhand pitch, throwing my phone into the other room before slamming both sets of doors and locking mine. I felt a grin forming on my lips. Leo double-checked the lock and then moved to the television and turned it on to a random music channel. He cranked the volume and finally turned back to me, his look decidedly determined.

My grin now fully in place, I gestured to the TV. "Is this your idea of mood music?" The stylings of Kenny G poured from the speaker.

He shrugged and kept coming at me. "Not really, but it's better than the sound of Malcolm delivering play-by-play commentary."

"Good point. Carry on." I opened my arms and he settled right back in, his nose running alongside mine and his warm breath fanning my cheek.

"God, I want you so badly, Ruby. Please say you want this too."

All I could do was nod before I found his mouth again, drawing in his minty taste and allowing my hands to explore his cotton-clad back. Any thought about the wisdom of engaging in hot sex with a man I'd just met and who would be crossing the ocean to a country his family freaking *ruled* went right out the window. All I could think about was the firmness of his shoulders and the press of his cock against my stomach.

It didn't take long for Leo's hands to travel down my back and find the hem of my oversized t-shirt. He ran the tips of his fingers over the skin just below my ass. I wasn't wearing a bra, and I think my subconscious had been planning on this interlude all along because I'd happened to pack my skimpiest pair of panties—a bright red thong with white polka dots on what little fabric there was. When Leo drew his fingers up and found my exposed ass cheeks, he groaned into my mouth so loud the vibration of it sent lightning down my spine and right to the center of me.

He took my ass in both hands and pulled me even closer into him while his fingers found the small barrier of cloth and slipped under it. It was my turn to groan but I pulled my mouth from his so I could breathe. Oxygen was a necessity, given my state of arousal.

"I need you to get those clothes off, Leo." My lips ran up his cheek and my fingers twisted in his shirt, threatening to rip the damn thing off him if he didn't comply within the next half a second.

He gave my ass a firm squeeze and released me long enough to pull the shirt over his head and unbuckle his belt. I worked on the button and zipper for him and had his jeans on the floor in record time. I didn't even look up for permission before yanking his boxers down as well. His cock practically sprang forward and I took it in my palm, drawing another loud groan.

"Jesus, Ruby." I looked up to find his head thrown back. I loved that my touch could undo him like this.

Not that I was given long to explore. Leo pulled me up to standing again. He reached for the hem of my shirt and lifted, forcing me to let go of his cock. And then he was bending me back to the bed, his mouth claiming one of my hardened nipples. I threaded my fingers through his hair, letting him know how highly I approved of our current activities. Although, I didn't object when he switched to the other breast and took that nipple between his teeth and bit down gently. My legs made an executive decision and wound around his waist, causing his cock to nestle in between my thighs, the swatch of polka dots the only thing separating us. I ground into him shamelessly.

Things went fast as lightning after that. My panties were a memory and Leo was pressing into me, his cock doing amazing things down south. We were a tangle of legs and hands, stroking and exploring every inch of each other's skin. The feel of him inside me was like nothing I'd ever experienced before. Leo's muscles strained under his skin with each thrust, lighting my sensitive nerve endings into a frenzy of want and need.

"Ruby. Ruby." He chanted my name in a breathless stream against my cheek as his cock worked to all but own me. Then his hand was pulling my leg up at the knee, changing the angle of his thrusts and hitting me in the one spot so perfect it had to have been named after God himself. In a show of appreciation, I screamed out both Leo's name and God's when I climaxed and pulsed wildly around Leo's hard cock as he continued to drive into me.

I was both a puddle of exhaustion and one giant exposed nerve, alternately shuddering and melting into the bed as Leo cried out his release into my hair and tensed every muscle in his body as it stilled over me. I wanted to freeze this moment and stay in this motel bed with this man's weight on top of me and his warmth spreading through me.

As the last tremble left Leo, he relaxed into me and nuzzled my hair. My hands stroked the bare skin of his back and my legs tightened around him again, keeping him inside me. He kissed my temple and ran his lips over to my cheek and mouth, dropping small kisses along the way. He was perfection. It was, without a doubt, the best sexual experience of my life. Leo Baxter had officially ruined me for other men.

And he'd be leaving in mere hours.

Driven by instinct, I squeezed him at the thought, making him chuckle into my mouth. I did the same, and he pulled back to look at me, both of us smiling like dopes and running our eyes over each other's faces, memorizing the features, the flush of skin, and the light sheen of sweat. We both completely rocked the post-awesome-sex look. Leo's thumbs stroked the hair at my temples and neither of us moved except to draw air into our lungs.

It hadn't escaped my attention that we'd been incredibly foolish and not used a condom, but I couldn't bring myself to regret it at the moment. Leo seemed to read my thoughts because he finally sighed and dropped his forehead to mine.

"I didn't use a condom." I couldn't sense regret in his tone either. It felt like a statement of satisfaction more than anything. It was another level of intimacy we shared, and as unwise as it was, it felt good.

"I know. I'm on the pill." I thought I owed it to him to let him know I wouldn't be chasing after him for child support next year. I guessed he was used to women being interested in his money and status more than the man he was. Stupid bitches. A twinge of guilt passed through me that I was kind of deceiving him by not letting on that I knew about the whole prince thing. But, honestly, it was way too easy to forget. He was Leo, the sweet boy who gave me a new definition of sexy and made me laugh and swoon. I wanted to know everything there was to know about him.

"In case you couldn't tell, that was amazing," I said. My lips curved and he lifted his head and smiled back at me.

"Just amazing? We may have to invent a new word to describe it."

"Phenometacular?" I offered.

He narrowed his eyes, thinking it over.

"Incredisome?"

"No. I like the first one better, but it still needs something."

I lifted my head and kissed his mouth. "Phenome-freaking-tacularly bitchin'."

"That's the one," he murmured against my mouth.

As enjoyable as it was to stay wrapped up in each other, Leo eventually untangled himself and went to the bathroom to clean up. He brought me back a warm washcloth and got a bit distracted cleaning me up. After his fifth, "Missed a spot," he had me giggling and squirming so much I could hardly breathe, so I had to roll him onto his back and pin him down on the bed. Not that he seemed to mind.

"So, Ruby Green, tell me more about you. I want to know everything." Again, it was as if he could read my mind. I traced his eyebrow with my fingertip, wanting to memorize everything.

"What else do you like to do besides fix up cars and rescue foreign guys?"

I thought about it for a minute. Truthfully, work and family took up most of my time. "Let's see. I like dancing, mostly to country music. Oh, and I love to cook."

"Oh, yeah? I'm pretty hopeless myself."

"At the dancing or the cooking?" My finger moved to the other brow.

"Dancing I can handle—although I've not done any country dancing." The vision of him line dancing had me pressing my lips together to hold back the laugh that was threatening. "I'm complete rubbish in the kitchen."

I tapped his nose. "Not to brag, but I'm kind of famous for some of my specialties."

"Color me impressed. Is there a big food scene in Kernersville?" His hand stroked my ass, making me temporarily lose focus.

"Nope. But there's a big food scene in the Green family."

He chuckled and brought his other hand down to join the first as I lay on top of him. "Okay, so what's your best dish?"

"Hands down, my Kickin' Chicken Cornbread Bake."

There came that brow V again. "That sounds ... kind of disgusting, to be honest."

I laughed at him. "It's like finding religion, I promise you."

"Well, then, you'll have to make it for me sometime. I've been meaning to find religion but I keep putting it off." Both our smiles fell as we realized the impossibility of us ever sitting down to that dinner.

"Ruby." My name was the only thing he could say.

I made myself smile. If I'd learned anything, it was to enjoy what you had because you never knew when it could be taken away from you. "So maybe we won't have my famous cornbread special, but I'd rather have this anyway." My palms settled on his chest as I sat and straddled his waist.

He gently brushed my nipples with the back of his hand. "You're so beautiful." His eyes came up to mine. "Thank you for this."

"For what? The hot sex? Believe me, the pleasure is all mine." I grinned.

He shook his head, a ghost of a smile on his lips. "No. Well, yes, of course, but more than that. You're a breath of fresh air. One I didn't even know I needed."

I leaned forward and dropped a kiss on his mouth. "In that case, you're welcome." I resettled myself over him. "What about you? What do you like to do besides build windmills and dig wells? And drive your electric car?" I made sure my lip curled at that.

"Hey. No making fun of my car."

"I really can't help it."

He growled and my lower belly tightened.

"Okay, let's see. I read quite a bit, I run whenever I can, and I have a slight addiction to American television. Our programming back home is lacking in variety."

"So you're kind of a homebody."

"I suppose so. Does that bother you?" He asked it as if we had a future to consider. My heart wanted to melt and break at the same time.

I just shook my head, not sure what to say. After a pause, I decided to dig in. "Okay, Leo, tell me something nobody else knows about you."

His lips twisted as he thought.

"Come on, there has to be something." I gave him a playful push from my position above him.

"I'm just trying to decide how you might be able to use it against me."

I gasped. "Seriously?"

He laughed and pulled me down for another kiss.

His words vibrated against my lips. "I've never been in love."

My heart galloped, a flood of emotions filling me. I

froze with my lips against his. To be loved by this man would be everything. It felt wrong that nobody had been on the receiving end of all Leo had to offer. It didn't matter that I'd known him for such a short time—my thoughts were the gut-level kind. And my gut was pretty damn trust-worthy. I tried to ignore the voice inside me that wanted to raise a hand and shout, "I volunteer!" Reality sucked sometimes.

There was no good way to respond to his confession, so I just kissed him again and sat back up.

"What about you?" His hands rested on my hips and his eyes swept over me. Good thing I wasn't a self-conscious woman or Leo would have had me blushing all day long.

"Me? I don't know. I thought I was in love once, but I was a teenager, so it didn't count. I mistook hormones and rebellion for love."

"Hmm." He considered that. "Actually, I meant to ask about something nobody else knows."

"Oh." I squinted, trying to come up with something. I generally liked to keep my shit to myself, so there were many directions I could go with my answer, but he'd shared a big one, so I felt it was only fair to reciprocate. Here went nothing. "My biggest fear is that I'll turn out like my mom." I'd never admitted that to anyone, not even Sadie.

Leo tilted his head. "How so?"

I shrugged. "She's missing that mom gene that makes a person care more about their kids than themselves. I'm terrified if I ever have kids, I'll be like her."

Leo shook his head. "But that's not possible."

I coughed out a laugh. "Are you psychic or something?"

"No, but I've seen you with Sadie and I've heard you

talk about your aunt and uncle. You're a family person through-and-through."

I took in his words. "Huh. I never really thought about it that way." I felt one side of my mouth turn up. "Maybe."

"I'd say definitely." He moved a hand to cover mine where it rested on his chest.

"Okay, this is getting way too deep," I declared. "We're moving on. Biggest pet peeve."

"Besides Malcolm?" he deadpanned.

I laughed.

"Probably when someone uses a Bluetooth device when talking on the phone and I think they're talking to me. I've embarrassed myself more than once with this."

I couldn't help the snicker. "I agree, and they look so self-important. It's just weird."

"What about you? What annoys you?" His hand squeezed mine.

My brows spiked. "The list is long, my friend. But if I had to pick one?" This was hard. "Okay, I can't. I think my top two are when someone clips their nails in public." I gave a fake shudder. "And when someone punches the damn elevator button right after I've just pushed it. I mean, do they think their fingers are freaking magic or something?"

Leo smiled, his eyes doing that sparkling thing again. "That's a good one. And I completely agree about the nail clipping. My sister used to sit next to me on the couch and clip her nails. Needless to say, I confiscated her clippers."

"First, ew. And second, you have a sister? You haven't mentioned her."

He looked surprised. "I haven't?" His head shook once.

"I suppose I've been too focused on the more troublesome sibling. Clara is much more pleasant than Malcolm, I can assure you."

I smiled at the image of Leo with the girl I'd seen in the photograph on Sadie's phone. It had to be her. She shared the same dark hair, that was clear, but I hadn't gotten a good look at her. My attention was otherwise occupied.

"Anyway, she's away at university, so I don't see her much except for the times she comes home for holidays and such."

"Do you live alone?"

He opened his mouth to answer and then closed it again, reconsidering. I wanted to cover my face. Stupid me. He probably lived in a damn castle with servants and staff lurking in every doorway, waiting to do his bidding. But, no. That didn't sound right. I couldn't reconcile that image with the man under me. I almost blurted out again that I knew. But I'd just had unprotected sex with him. Even I would question my motives at that point if I were him. Best to let it lie and just enjoy the time we had.

"I kind of share a place with a few other people," he finally said. Then, coming to a mistaken conclusion, he hurried to add, "But I don't have a girlfriend or anything of that sort!"

The thought hadn't even occurred to me. I hardly knew him, yet I knew to my core that Leo was not the cheating type. The almost pleading look in his eyes that I take him on his word had my heart turning over. I bent to kiss him again, taking my time about it until I was sure he was convinced we were *all* good.

"Well, good." I slid down his body a bit, feeling his hardness. "Because she'd be appalled by what I'm about to do to you."

CHAPTER SEVENTEEN

LEO

"Wait, so there's no alcohol in it?" Malcolm stared at the three bottles in front of him on the picnic table.

Ruby covered her eyes and shook her head. "Do you honestly think they'd serve it to children if there was?"

It was the morning after the most phenome-freaking-tacularly bitchin' night of my life, and the three of us sat outside at a rest stop on I-40, just west of Asheville. Ruby was conducting a lesson on American soft drinks, trying to explain the cultural significance to Malcolm, given his new obsession with Coca-Cola.

Mal shrugged and Ruby reached over and opened the bottle of something called Cheerwine before setting it back down next to the similar bottles of Pepsi and Coke. She was settled between my legs as I sat sideways on the wood seat, my arms around her waist. I honestly could not stop touching this woman.

We'd stayed up almost the whole night learning each other's bodies and what made the other one make interesting noises. I felt like I knew every inch of her by heart. In between all the sex and physical exploration, we lay awake in a tangle of sheets and limbs, sharing things about ourselves and finding more ways we clicked. The details of my identity were a thorn in my side and I vowed to tell her before the day was through. I knew bone-deep that I could trust her, and she was too open in her feelings to be faking any of her apparent fondness for me. It was time to let the entire truth out.

But first, we had something called soda to drink.

Ruby pointed to the Pepsi bottle. "See, here in the South, it's pretty much all about Pepsi. The only people who drink Coke are transplants from the North." She tapped the cap of the Coke bottle with her fingernail. "And because the headquarters are in Atlanta, I guess maybe people from Georgia. Then, of course, you have fast-food chains that serve it. But when it comes to local places, it's Pepsi in the South." She grabbed the bottle of Cheerwine and held it out to Malcolm. "But Cheerwine is a North Carolina classic."

Malcolm didn't look convinced. "You first." He gestured to both of us. Ruby didn't hesitate to lift the bottle to her lips and take a deep pull. I watched her throat and felt my jeans tighten as I remembered some of the things she'd done with that mouth of hers in the shower earlier that morning.

She licked her lips and winked at me, clearly knowing

exactly what she was doing to me. I didn't even think when she handed the bottle over. My eyes stayed on hers as I took a deep swallow of the drink and almost choked.

"Good God!" I coughed. "It's like diabetes in a bottle."

Ruby scowled and snatched the drink from my hand. "No it's not! It's delicious!"

I coughed again. "I forgot about your sweet tooth for a minute there." I wiped my mouth with the back of my hand.

"And don't forget my affection for all things cherry." She leaned in and gave me a brief kiss, letting the flavor of soda and Ruby settle on my lips. I gathered the taste with a swipe of my tongue.

"Is that what that is? Cherry flavor?" I savored the taste since it came from her.

"Yup. Cherry and a whole lot of bubbles. Yum." She took another sip and extended the bottle out to Malcolm who now wore a lazy grin as his gaze bounced back and forth between Ruby and me.

"Well, damn." His voice was quiet.

Ruby and I looked at each other and I shrugged, knowing that trying to explain my brother was like trying to explain dark matter—or Kanye West.

Malcolm finally grabbed the bottle and took a hesitant sip. He smacked his lips and studied the label. "Not bad. You know what would be great with this?" His eyes gleamed. "Some of Russell's moonshine."

Following the soda sampling, it was determined that we'd continue to Atlanta in search of Coke's birthplace. I didn't really care where we went, as long as I got more time with Ruby. Her ankle was doing a lot better, but she still didn't want to drive with it yet so Malcolm declared it was his turn. It wasn't that long of a drive anyway and, given his stomach's reaction to the mountain drive the day before, it was safest for all involved. Ruby also suggested we cut down south toward South Carolina to avoid the mountains just in case. Beautiful though they were, my eyes were on Ruby, so I couldn't have cared less.

She wore another one of those tops that tied behind her neck and exposed her shoulders. I sat in the backseat and she perched herself sideways so we could chat along the way. I wanted to talk to her alone but didn't know when the chance would present itself. There was no way I was broaching this delicate subject with Malcolm around.

He and I hadn't talked yet about when we'd be calling Trevor, and my stomach sank at the thought that the previous night may have been my last with Ruby.

"Hey, Mal, pass your phone over!" I rose my voice so he could hear me clearly. He handed it back to me without question. It was essentially a phone-shaped camera without service or wi-fi, but that was exactly what I wanted. Ruby gave me one of her inquisitive looks and I snapped a picture before she could blink.

"Wait! What are you doing?" She laughed and I snapped another one. Her hand reached for the phone but I held it back.

"At least get in the picture with me if you're going to keep clicking away." She rolled her eyes and I slid forward in the seat. We proceeded to be that disgusting couple who takes selfies like we're in a boardwalk photo booth. It was not a proud moment. But I couldn't regret it because, no matter what happened, I'd at least have physical proof that

Ruby existed and I had a perfect few days with her. It would have to be enough.

She ruffled my hair and laughed at me before planting a kiss on my cheek and shoving me back in my seat.

We were nearing the border to Georgia around lunchtime when Ruby came to the realization that we hadn't sampled any Carolina barbecue.

"I could get kicked out of North Carolina for not making you try it there, but luckily, we've got a treat in store for you before we leave South Carolina. It'll have to do." What was it about Americans forcing local food on us like they'd be incarcerated for not pushing regional specialties? She consulted her phone and directed us off I-85 into the town of Fair Play where we stopped at a lonely red-roofed building in the middle of some fields. It bore a sign reading The Spotted Pig. I thought it a bit morbid for a girl who didn't like to eat cute animals to march us into a restaurant with images and figures of the actual animal we'd be eating splashed all over, but she was a complex girl.

We got to choose our drinks, but Ruby took over when it came to ordering food. We soon found ourselves at a table filled with pulled pork, ribs, fried pickles, coleslaw, and something called hush puppies. Again with the cute animals thing. But Ruby assured me it was basically fried dough and had nothing to do with dogs. We'd be lucky to end this trip without suffering from heart failure with all the junk we'd been eating.

Ruby dug in unapologetically, getting barbecue sauce all over her hands and face as she tore at some ribs. Contrary to what I'm sure was normal, my base reaction was to get turned the hell on. She'd transformed me into a savage, and I couldn't have been more pleased.

"Oh, God," I moaned myself when I bit into a pulled pork sandwich. It was nothing short of amazing. And I didn't think I imagined the look in Ruby's eyes at my exclamation. It was like the sins of Lust and Gluttony were having their own party in The Spotted Pig and Ruby and I were the guests of honor. Good heavens.

Malcolm, lost in his own foodgasm, didn't seem to notice, thank God. When we were too full to fit even one more morsel of food, we tossed our napkins on the table and all went to wash up in the restrooms.

"I don't know if I've ever eaten that much in my life." Malcolm held his stomach as he waited for me to dry my hands.

"I'm thinking a nap is in order," I suggested. It wasn't as if I'd gotten adequate sleep the past several nights.

Malcolm groaned in agreement, leaning against the tile wall. "Speaking of, what do you say to another night's stay? I wouldn't have dared ask except with the way you and Ruby have been exchanging visual cunnilingus all day, I figured you'd jump at the idea."

I elbowed him firmly, but he wasn't lying. I'm sure Ruby and I had been almost unbearable to be around. After a minute, I finally responded, "I'm being entirely selfish on this, but yeah. Let's do it." I would owe Trevor, Alice, and the guys my first born by the time this was over.

"Excellent." Malcolm's smile spread from ear to ear as he clapped my shoulder. "I may get a room a few doors down this time, though."

I shoved him out the door in front of me.

Ruby was standing waiting for us, looking as gorgeous as ever in her denim skirt and red top. "You boys ready for Atlanta?"

"Lead the way."

"Are you sure you're okay with staying another night? You don't have to get back?" I pushed open the motel-room door and held it for Ruby. There was no doubt in my mind I wanted at least one more night with her if that was all I could have, but I thought I detected a shadow fall across her face when the three of us talked about it in the car after lunch.

But she just smiled at me. "Positive." She passed by me, limping a bit.

We'd chosen another somewhat run-down motel since they seemed to be the only ones that would accept Ruby's cleavage-and-cash deal. But I couldn't have cared less as long as she and I got to share the room. Malcolm was situating himself three doors down, a fact which made Ruby laugh instead of blush—yet another moment that made me want to pack her in my suitcase and take her home with me.

As soon as the door closed behind me, I approached her and pulled her into me. Her back arched as she lifted her head to meet my lips. We'd been behaving too well all day and it was damned exhausting. I needed to feel her skin against mine and my cock inside her as soon as humanly possible.

She pulled back breathlessly. "We don't have time.

We're meeting Malcolm in ten minutes." Regardless of her words, she leaned in for another kiss.

"He can sod off. I don't give a shit about Malcolm right now." I sucked her earlobe into my mouth and she rubbed the crotch of my jeans with her palm.

"I know, but I don't think I can focus on sex with him screaming, 'Coca-Cola time, bitches!' and banging on our door." Her hand shifted to better grip me through my jeans.

"I don't know what you've done to me. I've never needed someone this badly in my entire fucking life." I cupped her butt in my palms, letting my fingers drift to her inner thighs.

"I know." She moaned as I ground into her. "It's new to me too."

Then we stopped talking altogether and made out while barely keeping our clothes on until the fateful knock came.

"Stop fucking in there and get your arses out here. They close at five and I'm not missing this so you two can get each other off all afternoon. Plenty of time for that later!" We heard him add in a softer tone, "Sorry, ma'am. Didn't see you there."

This made Ruby and me laugh, and we managed to pull apart, both of us looking more than a little rumpled.

Ruby opened the door for Malcolm while I adjusted myself. "Do come in."

"I was almost beaten with an old woman's handbag," Malcolm said and then frowned when he noted the state we were both in. "How is this fair?"

Ruby patted him on the head and went to use the loo.

We let Malcolm lead the way once we arrived at World of Coca-Cola. There were some interesting exhibits and even a tasting room, but it was a bit like two adults taking their rambunctious child to a carnival. By late in the afternoon, Ruby and I were exhausted, so we sat beside one another waiting for Malcolm to get his turn at a hands-on exhibit. Luckily, he hadn't pushed any small children out of his way.

"Your brother is one interesting guy."

I laughed. "That's one way of putting it." If she only knew. I got up from my chair. "I'm going to run and get a water. You want one?"

Ruby smiled that dazzling smile and shifted her eyes back to Malcolm. "Sure. I'll keep an eye on the little prince."

I froze.

What had she just said?

I watched her face for a moment. She laughed at something Malcolm was doing, but my eyes stayed on her. I didn't know what to do. Should I ask her to repeat herself? No. She'd definitely said "the little prince." But that could be a coincidence, right? He was acting like a kid. But that term was fairly specific. Wasn't it?

Shit.

"Be right back," I said and rushed away. I needed a minute alone to think before I fucked everything up. My feet took me to the lobby where I paced back and forth. I retraced every moment with Ruby since we'd met, looking for clues that she knew all along. She clearly hadn't known that first night when she was ready to beat both of us up. But what about the next morning? She could have easily looked me up since she had a damn picture of my ID. How could I be so stupid?!

But I'd been deceiving her too, hadn't I? I mean, the very thought of holding my true identity back from her had been gnawing at me. I was basically a hypocrite.

I took a deep breath and paced some more, drawing curious glances and not giving one shit. We needed to talk —that's what it boiled down to. It wasn't as if I hadn't already been planning this conversation all day. We'd go back to the motel and have an honest conversation, getting it all out in the open. My stomach pitched as a mental image of Ruby surfaced. Her open, genuine nature was so alluring. Was it possible it was all an act? And if so, to what end?

By the time we arrived back at the motel, I was a coiled spring ready to release. Ruby had been shooting me looks ever since I returned to the table and suggested we get ourselves moving to miss the rush-hour traffic. Luckily, Malcolm hadn't put up a fight. His Coke fix had been met so he was content to go back to the motel and take a nap before dinner. I wasn't sure I could stomach anything, but I supposed the night's events hinged on the outcome of my talk with Ruby.

Malcolm ambled over to his door while Ruby and I went to ours. Before I even inserted the key, I turned to face her. Her eyes were huge gray pools, framed by concerned brows. God, she was so stunning. I begged for this to be a huge misunderstanding and for any potential issues to dissipate into thin air. But, what was I really hoping for, anyway? I was leaving—probably in a few short hours.

"We need to talk," I blurted out more loudly than I meant to.

Her mouth turned down. "Um. Okay." She tucked her hair behind one ear. "I thought you seemed kind of ... off on the ride back."

I just nodded and opened the door. We both set our things down and Ruby turned back to me. "Let me go to the bathroom real quick and then we can sit and talk, okay?" She took a deep breath. What was she preparing to say during our talk?

She disappeared behind the door and I sat on the bed taking deep breaths of my own. As if fate were making a sport of fucking with us, that damn annoying ringtone came blaring from Ruby's phone where it lay in her open purse. I clenched my teeth as I waited it out and the ringing finally silenced. My nerves were raw.

So when a text notification dinged immediately after, followed by two more, I caved and lifted the phone from her purse.

Three text messages stared back at me from the screen.

Nash: *Missed you last night. Call me ASAP.*

Nash: *I don't have to tell you how happy I am that you changed your mind about things.*

Nash: *Can't wait to have you back in my bed.*

I read them again, and then one more time to be sure I hadn't possibly misread. But I hadn't.

Ruby had been lying to me all along. Not only that, but she had a fucking *boyfriend.* She was playing me and Malcolm from the beginning with her openness and generosity, and she was one hell of a good actress. Either she was planning on taking us for all the money she could, or she was going to out us and try to cash in that way. I couldn't believe how stupid I'd been! Her trip to the bathroom with her cousin—if that's who Sadie even was—had to have been some part of the scheme. Had they traded recordings or photos? Were pictures of my brother and me on their way to reporters back home already? God, and Malcolm in that t-shirt. Good lord! Mother would skin us alive. The shirt alone was a PR nightmare. I couldn't even begin to think about the rest of the things she'd witnessed and possibly recorded.

Our night together! Fuck! Had she made a sex tape? And the condom! Of course, she'd said she was on the pill. What kind of idiot was I?! My heart was beating out of my chest and I thought I might vomit. Mal and I had to get out of here.

But if I confronted her now, without giving our PR people some time to prepare, things would be even worse. I carefully replaced the phone in her purse and scrubbed my hands through my hair, trying like hell to calm down. If she saw me like this she'd know.

But this was *Ruby*. The Ruby I knew would never be capable of anything of this nature. She didn't have a disloyal or shallow bone in her body.

That was just it, though, wasn't it? The Ruby I knew didn't exist. She was an imaginary girl who'd swooped in and turned my world upside down and stolen my heart. But she was only a shadow, not real at all.

I didn't hesitate. I didn't think. I just pulled Ruby's phone back out and dialed Trevor's number.

CHAPTER EIGHTEEN

RUBY

I took a deep breath and opened the door, completely unsure what to expect. Leo, looking ridiculously long, lean, and sexy in dark-wash jeans and his Captain America t-shirt—which was becoming a personal favorite—lay back against the headboard of the whitewashed bedframe. His eyes were closed and I thought for a second he was asleep. Not that I blamed him. I was exhausted. Last night had been the most rigorous workout of my life, and I ached in all sorts of wonderful places. This was a price I was more than willing to pay for the experience.

Leo blinked, and I saw strain around his eyes. "You okay?" I climbed on the bed and waited for him to put an arm out to invite me into the warm crook he had between his arm and chest. My head fit perfectly there, resting just under his chin. But he didn't. Something was definitely wrong.

We'd closed ourselves in this little bubble of sex and happiness, but the real world wouldn't stay at bay forever. I groaned inwardly at the thought of the call I owed Nash, not to mention Carl and Sadie. I assumed we'd be returning to reality in the morning. Was that what Leo wanted to talk about? Was it what had him looking unsettled.

Leo blinked a few more times and studied my face like he was trying to memorize it. I stayed silent, not sure what to say or do. Finally, he shook his head and let out a breath. "I think that lunch isn't agreeing with me." He put a hand to his gut.

Oh.

"Yeah, I think I'm going to pass on dinner if that's okay with you?" He didn't sound right.

"I thought you wanted to talk about something."

He shook his head again. "It can wait. Really, it's no big deal."

I shifted on the bed but Leo just closed his eyes again. Maybe he really was just feeling sick. I got up and walked to the other side of the bed and bent down to kiss his temple. He startled and I jerked back. This was so strange. What had happened to the easy comfort we had? The intimacy? It had been less than an hour since we flirted shamelessly at the Coke facility and I missed it more than was probably healthy.

"Why don't you get some sleep? I'm sure you'll feel better after a nap." I stepped back awkwardly. "I'll give you some quiet and go hassle your brother for a bit." I attempted to joke, but only a corner of his lips twitched up, and it seemed unnatural at best.

Crap.

I grabbed my purse and quietly left the room, catching one last glimpse of Leo before the door clicked shut.

Malcolm frowned at his plate. "God, you're bossy, aren't you?"

Despite the distraction of thoughts of Leo, I managed a smile. "I'm only looking out for you." I pointed to the salad I'd made him order. "I don't want your arteries closing in on themselves and killing you before you get home."

The waitress grinned at my comment and asked if we needed anything else before moving to another table. I took a large sip of my Pepsi.

"I'm fairly certain you get the guillotine for killing the future king—death by barbecue or not."

I choked and spit my mouthful of soda all over the table, a good portion landing on Leo's salad.

"Oh good," he said, pushing the plate aside. "Now I don't have to eat it."

I coughed some more. "Wh-what did you just say?"

He took his napkin and focused on wiping up the fizzy liquid. "Oh, come on, Ruby. You heard exactly what I said."

I finished coughing into my napkin and then switched to water, gulping down half my glass before even attempting to meet Malcolm's eyes. When I finally did, they were both knowing and soft. I swallowed thickly. "Does Leo know?"

He shook his head, and something deep inside me sighed with relief. Nevertheless, I shook my head. "It's not what you think, Malcolm."

He reached across the table and put a hand on my arm. "Look, I know I come off as a bit unfocused, but I'm an observant guy. I know exactly what's going on."

"But—" I tried to interject, but Malcolm continued.

"You're not doing anything wrong. Your cousin told you who we were and you decided to leave us our privacy. I actually wanted to thank you."

My nose scrunched up. "Thank me?"

He leaned back in his seat looking at me with eyes that were way too familiar. "Yeah. I needed this break, and Leo needed to lighten up. You helped out with both."

"Seriously?" It was my turn to lean back and take him in.

"Absolutely. I've been dreading going home. I'm not sure how much you know, but it's complicated."

I nodded and tried sipping my soda again. Small sips this time.

"Anyway, Leo's always wound way too tight. He's a workaholic and has no social life to speak of. Then he laid eyes on you."

I couldn't help the smile forming on my lips.

"You've done what I've been completely unable to."

I gasped in feigned shock. "Well, I should hope not."

Malcolm grinned and pointed at me. "See that, right there. You're a fucking delight. You draw Leo out, and you're good for him."

I shifted in my seat and played with my straw. "How can you be so sure I'm not after something from you guys?"

He laughed—right in my face. "Ruby, I never knew what the phrase 'wearing your heart on your sleeve' meant until I met you. You're an open book."

Hmm. I wasn't so sure about that. There was a lot I was hiding.

"So, what happens now? I'm assuming we tell Leo I know."

Malcolm threw out a hand. "No way."

"But I've already been feeling bad about lying to him. Shouldn't I tell him?"

Malcolm was shaking his head. "You don't understand. When people know who we are, they treat us differently. It's impossible to tell who's being genuine and who's after something. We've both been burned one time too many."

I'd guessed as much, but it was still upsetting to hear.

"Leo's way too guarded. But he's not that way with you. As soon as he finds out you know, he'll close himself off. He won't be open to ... possibilities."

I didn't know what kind of possibilities Malcolm was talking about, but I supposed it didn't matter all that much after all. They'd be leaving before I knew it.

As if responding directly to my thoughts, Malcolm said, "But I need to go home. I've been avoiding it as long as I can, but my father's ill and I need to finish preparing to take his place."

I shook my head. "I can't believe you're going to be a real live king." I knew that sounded stupid, but I didn't know how else to say it. This flighty, funny, ill-mannered boy was going to rule a nation.

"That makes two of us."

"So, can I ask, what was with the 'roughing it' routine?

No clothes, no phones, no car? Surely you could have traveled in style—I mean, not that anything could be more stylish than Stella, of course."

He grinned again. "Our head of security was tracking us so we had to ditch everything. He's a sneaky bastard."

"I assume he's the Trevor guy who was on his way to the garage when we skipped town in Kernersville?"

"The very same. Leo had a burner phone and called him with it. He was firmly on team 'Go home' until you batted your eyes at him."

I flipped him off, making his grin spread. I looked around for the waitress so I could order Malcolm another salad.

"I'm actually shocked he hasn't caught up with us since. Trevor is part bloodhound."

I froze. All thoughts of healthy greens flew from my head as an idea occurred to me. I turned back to Malcolm who was staring at the fries on my plate like they were his "Precious." I snapped my fingers to get his attention and his eyes shot to me. "So, what are your feelings on granting favors to women who drive kick-ass cars?"

He eyed me with a mischievous glint. "I'm highly in favor."

Thank God.

By the time we got back to the motel, my outlook had brightened considerably. Malcolm and I had determined that Leo's mood change was most likely due to some guilt he had at not telling me about the whole prince thing—although, we didn't discount the possibility of barbecue overload either.

Dinner had been a giant adrenaline rush, and I was looking forward to finding a spot on the bed next to Leo and crashing. We could always wake up early and make up for lost time. To that end, I tried to be as quiet as possible when I opened the door. Sure enough, Leo was exactly where I'd left him, but his shoes lay on the floor and he'd thrown the bedding over himself. I crept over to the bed, drinking in his features as they sat relaxed in sleep. It was amazing how I'd just spent the last hour sitting across from an identical face, yet not one of Malcolm's features had my belly doing high dives. I wanted to run my finger across his forehead and trace his nose and lips, but he looked so peaceful, I didn't dare wake him.

After what was probably a creepy length of time, I made my way to the bathroom and got ready for bed. I refused to think about this being our last few hours together, and instead focused on not waking Leo as I climbed in beside him and gently put an arm around his stomach, my head settling on his Captain America shoulder, trying to worm its way into that crook. I yawned and then laid a gentle kiss on Leo's chest before dropping off to sleep.

Despite my best intentions, I knew by the light streaming through the crack in the curtains that it was full morning when I awoke. My first thought was that Leo and I had better start getting it on if we hoped to at least take the edge off before check-out time. But that thought faded to dust as the realization that my arms were encircling a pillow and not a hot man-chest hit me full force. I blinked and rubbed my eyes before looking around the room. Leo was nowhere to be seen. Even the bathroom door was wide open and the lights were off.

Had he gone for a coffee run? That was probably the case. And, knowing him, he'd bring back something sweet too. The thought had a smile touching my lips.

I hopped out of bed, testing my ankle and finding it even better than the day before. There was no way I was kissing Leo with this morning breath so I headed to the bathroom to brush my teeth. But something was very wrong. When I flipped on the light, there were only two items on the countertop. My cosmetic bag and a neatly-formed stack of bills that looked a lot larger than the one I'd seen at my apartment.

I approached as if it could be a booby trap. What the hell was this? Sure enough, the top bill was $100 and I was guessing the rest were the same. I turned and rushed to the door of our room. Sunlight nearly blinded me when I swung the door open and whipped my head around, trying to take in the entire parking lot at once. Even with spots in my eyesight, I saw Stella immediately. I quickly propped the door open and strode down to Malcolm's room as fast as my ankle would allow. After a full minute of pounding and no response, I put my back to the door and sank down onto the concrete.

They'd left. Leo had left. And he hadn't even said goodbye.

~ This is the end of *Between a Rock and a Royal* (*Kings of Carolina*, Book 1) ~

Continue reading for a peek at Book 2, *Blue Bloods and Backroads*.

LEO

Rain formed fast-moving rivers on the airplane window as we ascended to our cruising altitude. The shitty weather was apropos, given the general tone of our day. I felt rather than saw Malcolm settle in one of the seats across from me.

"Is it strange that I miss the cramped quarters of that Mustang's backseat?"

I sent him my worst glare. Insensitive prick.

He put his hands up in defense

Why he would try to provoke me, I had no idea. The morning had been a whirlwind of bad gone to worse.

It had started with me waking from a dream where I was chasing Ruby down the street as she drove Stella away, pieces of gravel spitting from beneath her tires and pinging against the bumper. Once my eyes opened, I realized the pinging sound was coming from the window of our room. I was about to jump out of bed when the feel of Ruby's arm over my stomach registered. I looked down to see her settled with her head of glossy gold and bronze hair on my shoulder and I could feel her warm, steady breath against my neck. Every part of me instinctively began to curl into her—until the previous day's revelations hit me. I gently extracted myself and walked to the window where I pulled the curtain back. It was dark, but the dim light outside our door perfectly illuminated Trevor's face—Trevor's livid face.

I held up a finger and let the curtain fall back in place, taking a peek back at the bed to make sure Ruby was still out. Key in hand, I gingerly opened the door and crept outside, careful to ease it shut again. With a finger to my lips, I ushered a red-faced Trevor to a spot across the car park. He, surprisingly, followed without comment. There was no sign of Alice or anyone else, which I found odd.

"You have no bloody idea what it took not to bang down your door, Your Highness."

I nodded. "I know. And I apologize. But the girl is in there and we couldn't risk waking her."

Trevor's jaw ticked and he looked to his feet, probably trying to rein in his anger so he didn't strangle me right there in the car park. "About that, Sir. I've already alerted the appropriate people and they're trying to put a stop to anything before it can be published. I'm waiting for an update. But there's something else."

My stomach dropped. I hadn't told Trevor about the entire range of possible leaks yet, just a basic overview that we were probably screwed. But his next words had thoughts of potential scandals disappearing into thin air.

"It's your father."

My head became light. "What happened?"

"He took a bad fall." Trevor put his hands out to stop me from interrupting. "He'll be okay, but you and Prince Malcolm need to get home *now*."

I nodded. "Absolutely. Let me grab Malcolm." I took off for Malcolm's room before Trevor could say another word, not caring that my feet were bare and rocks bit into my soles. This was what happened when we didn't take our positions seriously, when we were reckless and threw caution to the wind. We didn't have that liberty, Malcolm nor I. We were going home, and I only hoped we could clean up the mess we'd made. It was time to leave America and go back to reality.

Continue reading **Blue Bloods and Backroads** (*Kings of Carolina*, Book 2) by purchasing a copy from your favorite retailer.

Don't forget to sign up for my newsletter for all the latest in my world of sexy romantic comedies!
bit.ly/news-from-sylvie

Thank you so much for reading *Between a Rock and a Royal*. This one was a bit of a departure for me since I usually write "everyday folk" and not wealthy royals, but it was so fun to write. I hope you enjoyed it! If you did, a **review** on your favorite book site is always appreciated!

Want to hang out with me? Join my **Reader Group** on Facebook: www.facebook.com/groups/SylviesSpot

Want to stay updated on new releases, promotions and giveaways? Subscribe to my newsletter by hopping on over to my website www.sylviestewartauthor.com.

Stay up to date and keep in touch!

- www.sylviestewartauthor.com
- sylvie@sylviestewartauthor.com

- Facebook: SylvieStewartAuthor
- Twitter: @sylvie_stewart_
- Instagram: sylvie.stewart.romance

XOXO,
Sylvie

My life is a friggin' fairytale—just not the kind any single girl would ever want to star in.

LANEY:

Like any good heroine, I have challenges to face. Getting my son to wear pants is one; dealing with my snooze-fest of a job is another. Then there's the Beast, my freeloading brother who's worn a permanent dent in the couch at my new place. And no fairytale would be complete without a smoking hot prince, of course. Too bad he's a complete ass.

My instincts scream at me to steer clear of Nate Murphy. Because, if life has taught me anything, there is no such thing as happily ever after.

NATE:

I may not be a superhero, but I do my best to come to the

rescue when I'm needed. And, hey, I just moved halfway across the country after a single phone call from my mom. But being back home and taking on the responsibilities involved makes me a bit cranky at times. Unfortunately, the one time I completely lose my cool is in front of the hottest girl I've ever met. I've got my work cut out for me if I'm going to fix this. But I *will* fix this.

I'll be anything Laney Monroe needs me to be ... a super-hero, a prince, or just a guy she might take a chance on.

Grab your copy of **The Fix** and start the award-winning Carolina Connections series today!

USA Today bestselling author Sylvie Stewart is addicted to Romantic Comedy and Contemporary Romance, and she's not looking for a cure. She hails from the great state of North Carolina, so it's no surprise that her books are mostly set in the Tar Heel state. She's a wife to a hilarious dude and mommy to ten-year-old twin boys who tend to take after their father in every way. Sylvie often wonders if they're actually hers, but then she remembers being a human incubator for a gazillion months. Ah, good times.

Sylvie began publishing when her kids started elementary school, and she loves sharing her stories with readers and hopefully making them laugh and swoon a bit along the way. If she's not in her comfy green writing chair, she's probably camping or kayaking with her family or having a glass of wine while binge-watching Hulu. Or she's been kidnapped—so what are you doing just sitting there?!!

**Winner of the 2017 National Indie Excellence Award for Romantic Comedy

**Winner of the 2017 Readers' Favorite Silver Medal for Romantic Comedy

facebook.com/SylvieStewartAuthor

twitter.com/sylvie_stewart_

instagram.com/sylvie.stewart.romance

bookbub.com/authors/sylvie-stewart

www.ingramcontent.com/pod-product-compliance
Lightning Source LLC
Chambersburg PA
CBHW070319190726
48291CB00014B/2355